TAMING
THE ALPHA
ZARA HOFFMAN

ZH
press

For June and Julie

part one

When the snows fall and the white winds blow,
The lone wolf dies but the pack survives.

GEORGE R.R. MARTIN

CHAPTER 1

DYLAN STARED AT THE TEXT NOTIFICATION AND SWALLOWED the lump in his throat. He'd been dodging Fawn for a while. He hadn't gone to her wedding five years ago and the last time he'd spent any quality time with her was at her brother's wedding three years ago. She'd been his first love and would always have a special place in his heart. He was happy she had found her other half. He really was. But seeing her with Caleb still made him a little sad. Maybe it was because he knew the angel was her true soulmate—something he could never compete with. He still couldn't be around them without being a little jealous. And that was what made him a coward.

He jumped when he felt a kiss on his cheek. Bailey stood next to him and he realized he'd been standing still lost in his thoughts too long. She went to grab the card, but he raised it over her petite frame, out of reach. He realized his mistake too late.

Her dark eyes flashed with frustration. "It's the witch, isn't it? What's she done now? Does she need us to fight another battle for her?"

After his Pack had joined the fight against the hordes of Hell infiltrating New York, she still insisted Fawn thought wolves were a disposable army. The past few years had done nothing to diminish Bailey's disdain for the Belgrave family. He'd given up on convincing Bailey that they weren't the callous users she was determined to condemn them as. "She's getting married."

"Good for her."

Dylan heard a bite to her voice. When they'd met a few years ago, Bailey had gone possessive, throwing their relationship in both Fawn's and Ivy's faces. Neither of them was a fan of her since, but Ivy had taken it worse and fought back.

His girlfriend continued, "Why does that have you stewing? Don't tell me you still have feelings for her?"

He still didn't fully understand how Bailey hadn't heard his kitchen confession with Fawn when Caleb had, but he wasn't about to fill her in. He was slightly embarrassed he'd told Fawn he still loved her after so many years. And he felt a bit guilty for doing it when he knew she and her soulmate were on rocky ground. "No." At least, he didn't think he did. But his current feelings toward Fawn, whatever they were, weren't his reasoning for what he had to do next. He took a deep breath, "Bailey, I don't think we're good together anymore—"

She cut him off. "If you're going to break up with me, just say it." Her mouth curled into a sneer. "You're pathetic, Dylan. You can't keep pining over her. She's a witch and you're a werewolf. It could never work. I don't know what you thought would happen."

Her words hurt, but they weren't strictly untrue. While it was possible for wolves to have non-werewolf soulmates, it was uncommon, and even more rare for an Alpha to have a non-wolf Mate. But her tone was unacceptable. He might not yet be the official Alpha yet, but it was still his responsibility to maintain order.

"Careful, Bailey," he warned, his voice dropping. "You can be angry with me, but you're still a member of my father's Pack—the one that I'll be in charge of one day. Show the proper respect. As I was saying, I think we should break up."

She glared at him but didn't say anything. She left the common room and slammed the house's back door.

He sighed, thankful she hadn't thrown the one thing that could undermine his leadership in his face: without a Mate, no werewolf could be an Alpha. The Council made annual visits to every Pack to ascertain that the sons of current Alphas had been successfully united with their other half. Every year when they came to him, he could see the disappointment on their faces. They had always liked his father, and the idea of letting his father and them down chafed at him. Perhaps that was the reason they had given him more time, rather than the official statement that any future Alpha has until his father's death or stepping down to find his Mate.

"What's up her ass?"

Dylan turned to see his best friend within the Pack. Edon was the son of his father's Beta, Connor, and since he had moved to New Orleans, they had been inseparable. It was different than how he'd been with Alec, but Pack bonds were much more involved than human friendships, so it was truly impossible to compare.

They were as close as brothers and were often mistaken as such by strangers who saw them hanging out in the Quarter. At first glance, the only obvious difference between was Edon's dark hair in comparison to his blond locks. When they'd been in college together, being mistaken for brothers had also garnered them extra interest in female best friends who dreamed of having double-weddings. Of course, none of them had been their Mates, so it didn't matter. Once Edon found Annabelle, that was it for him. The same way it was for every wolf who found their Mate. The world revolved around their other half, and everyone else paled in comparison.

"I broke up with her. She may have bared her teeth at me."

That got Edon's attention. "I'll handle it." He started for the door, but Dylan called him back.

"Calm down." He appreciated Edon's defensiveness on his behalf, but sometimes his Beta had a hotter head than him. And when the adviser was less level-headed than the leader he was supposed to be aiding, it wasn't the best situation. "I gave her a warning. I don't need her publicly punished or kicked out over this."

"I can't believe you're protecting her. She's always been a rotten person. I wish our dads would have kicked her out once her parents died. At least *they* knew how to behave."

"She wasn't always like this. She changed after she lost her mate."

His friend let out a low growl, but Dylan knew it wasn't directed at him.

"Let's go for a perimeter sweep." Despite being a flat landscape, the Morsure territory was covered in trees and too large to see the boundary, even with enhanced werewolf vision. "Tell the others the last one back has to do the laundry this week."

ZELDA GLANCED AT THE CLOCK HANGING ABOVE THE bar. Her feet ached, but she steeled herself. She could make it the last fifteen minutes of her shift and close for the night. She hated traveling back to the hotel on her own at two in the morning, but it's what she had to do to pay the bill. The smell of fryer grease and beer permeated the air no matter how many times the place was cleaned, her werewolf nose would always be able to pick up the smell.

"Zelda," her boss called, "I need you for a moment."

She glanced around the mostly empty restaurant. All of the customers had been given their checks and paid but they clearly wanted to close out the place.

Zelda stashed the rag under the bar on her way to the office.

He closed the door behind her and motioned her to take a seat. His hand trembled slightly, and he was oddly quiet. Something was wrong.

She lowered herself into the chair, eyeing him, and waited for him to say something.

"I'm selling the business."

It didn't take a genius to figure out what was coming next.

"The new owners are coming tomorrow to start renovations, and they want to hire their own employees."

"I understand." She knew the restaurant hadn't been doing so well lately, and she didn't blame her boss or even the new owners for making their business decisions. But without a job, how was she supposed to support her Pack?

He reached into a drawer and pulled out a lockbox. She squashed her curious instinct to look inside as he pulled something out.

He passed her a white envelope with her name written in his scratchy handwriting. "Your pay for your double shifts this week. I threw in a little extra. I really am sorry, Zelda."

"Thank you. What will you do now?"

"Enjoy retirement. It came sooner than I planned, but I'm looking forward to relaxing."

She hung up her apron and stuck the money in the inner pocket of her coat. She left with the customers when it was closing time.

Zelda walked quickly on the dark and mostly deserted streets. She was tempted to Shift and get back to her Pack as soon as possible, but it was too dangerous. It might be the middle of the night, and she could probably find an alley to hide during the process, but the pain was always just this side of unbearable that it took all her physical and mental strength to keep from screaming as each of her bones broke and reformed into the form of a wolf.

She had learned early, after her second time, that expressing pain during Shifting marked you as weak. The excruciating process never got easier, only faster. There was no way around the pain. Wolves just got better at containing themselves.

Without a job, they were going to have to move. Again. She hated regularly relocating, as did her Pack members, but they had no choice. Her arrogant brother, Liekos, had guaranteed their vagrant lives when he challenged the Waya Pack in a territory dispute. He'd not only lost their home, but also his life. He'd always been a little too arrogant, but since their father died, he had gotten so much worse.

She'd had her doubts. But unlike their father, who was open to constructive criticism by the other wolves in his Pack, Liekos didn't listen to anyone except his yes-man Beta. If he weren't her brother and her Alpha, she'd have killed him herself.

Now without territory, accidentally trespassing on other Packs' land was an unavoidable evil to contend with, but she couldn't afford to lose any of her other Pack members. She was responsible for their well-being and she had to prove that she could succeed where her brother had failed.

She ducked into the small motel that she had been able to buy out for their Pack. She opened her door and groaned when her best friend, and now Beta, was waiting inside.

"You okay?" he asked.

"What do you think, Raoul?"

His expression darkened. "What happened?"

"I got laid off."

He stood and started for the door. "I'll make them pay."

She blocked the exit. "*No*, you won't. It wasn't personal or malicious. My boss is selling the place." She pulled the money out of her coat. "He paid me for the week, but it's not enough to keep living here. I need you focused on helping me figure out the next step."

He kept approaching, looking ready to move her aside if necessary.

"Stop it," she repeated. "That's an order from your Alpha, Raoul."

He stopped, but she could tell he wasn't happy about it. He blew out a breath, something he only did when he was pissed off.

She sighed. "I know we used to joke about starting our own Pack, but this wasn't what I had in mind." She sighed. *It was never meant to happen at all.* Although they'd always been the closest of friends, she knew that he didn't see her *that* way, and she never had anything more than friendly feelings toward him either. "I don't have any idea what I'm doing. And the money to stay here runs out after tonight. We're going to have to relocate. Again."

He nodded. "I can tell the Pack first thing tomorrow if you want." His expression turned thoughtful. "You should go to sleep. You look like you're about to fall down." As the second son of her father's Beta, she knew he was responsible enough to handle the job.

"They should hear it from their Alpha."

"I'll be there when you do." His tone brooked no argument, but she wasn't about to tell him no. She needed the support.

She got up and knocked on all the other doors, Raoul walking behind her. Each group of wolves looked groggy and suspicious. She told everyone the same thing. "We have to relocate tomorrow, so get your things ready before going back to sleep. We leave first thing in the morning."

One question rang out over and over. *Where are we going?*

"We're going to New Orleans." Zelda wasn't sure what made her say that, but she remembered her father once mentioning he'd made a friend with a fellow Alpha he had met in New York, and that he'd relocated to Louisiana's famous city. Maybe he could help her.

She needed to save her Pack before they assumed she was as bad as her brother at leading. Or, even more insulting, insisted she find her Mate so he could become their Alpha, stripping her of her last connection to her family's legacy of leading the Equinox Pack.

That would happen over her dead body.

CHAPTER 2

DYLAN HAD JUST FINISHED HIS SCAN OF THE perimeter of their territory near the lake when Edon's voice boomed through his head.

Rogues at the river! The warning resounded through his mind as he spun on his paws and took off running toward his Beta's call. Edon had taken three of the Pack's members with him, and he had the other two who'd joined their run.

With his father out of town for the week, Alec was responsible for their safety. *Contain them, but don't engage until I get there.* He motioned for the two members with him to go ahead. If the threat was a large one, he needed his patrol there to deal with it. Rogues were rare, especially a group of them. He wouldn't have them attack unless it was necessary, but he needed to be prepared.

When he arrived, his Pack had successfully encircled twelve werewolves. Each of them carried a small satchel in their mouths. They were on the run from something. Standing in front of them, and slightly apart, was a male and a female. The Alpha and his Luna.

We need your help, the female wolf said.

Dylan nodded his head then glanced at the male. *Does your Luna always speak first?*

The other wolf growled. *Don't disrespect* Alpha *Makris.*

Dylan tilted his head, focusing on Alpha Makris. Now that he saw her, he couldn't seem to bring himself to look away. *I didn't mean to offend you, Alpha Makris. You have my sincerest apologies. My name is Dylan Stone, Alpha of the Morsure Pack.*

Temporary and future Alpha, Edon's voice reminded him. It was times like this when he was glad Alphas and Betas could privately communicate. He'd have probably died from embarrassment long ago if everyone in the Pack heard everything his father and best friend had ever telepathically told him. It would negate mental communication altogether.

Dylan ignored him. Another beat passed and Makris' Beta stopped growling. She must've said something to him.

Dylan took the Beta's silence and Makris' attentive ears as permission to continue. *I don't know why you've brought your Pack here, but I invite you into our compound as temporary guests until you tell me why you're here.*

Are you sure this is a good idea? Edon's voice filtered into his mind as he led the way back to the house. *What if they're in trouble? Our Pack can't be responsible for that.*

He should have been thinking of her whole Pack, but his mind was fixated on making sure she was okay. And there was only one explanation he could think of. But if she *was* his Mate, wouldn't he know immediately? He'd always heard it was the most literal version of "love at first" sight. It wasn't supposed to leave any doubt. Even if her Beta wasn't already glaring daggers at him, he couldn't very well confirm his suspicion by getting closer to her without starting a fight.

Dylan finally answered Edon. *They're friends until proven enemies, remember?* When his friend looked skeptical, he took a deep breath. *I'll figure it out*, he added, trying not to snap.

He knew Edon was right, but the reminder of his temporary leadership wasn't helpful at the moment.

He led everyone to the house, holding the door open. His patrol walked through first, followed by the members of the Equinox Pack.

The last person inside was Alpha Makris, and Dylan had to blink at her beauty. It was as if his whole world tipped over the moment her golden eyes met his gaze, and he knew what that meant. He'd been right at the riverbank. She was the one he'd been looking for.

Head reeling, Dylan finally understood how every wolf felt once in their lifetime. After years of having no way to find his Mate, fate had dropped her at his doorstep.

ZELDA FELT LIKE SOMEONE HAD KNOCKED HER ON her ass. And that hadn't happened since she was twelve when Raoul had landed a lucky shot on her during a sparring session. Her father had congratulated him and gently, but firmly, told her to stay sharp. She had followed his advice ever since. If only he had done the same.

She mentally shook herself. Looking at the Alpha of the Morsure Pack made her feel as if she could barely draw her next breath. She'd always scoffed at stories of Mates becoming breathless at the first meeting. How wrong she had been. She knew Raoul was probably waiting for her inside, but all she could focus was on Alpha Stone. Wolves weren't known for being generous to strangers, much less Alphas, but this man had already opened his home to her and her Pack without any explanation from her. Was he really that kind or was it because he already knew they were Mates and it was merely out of obligation? That dampened the elation she'd been feeling, throwing her back into her harsh reality.

He cleared his throat and she willed her feet to move. She tried her best to walk inside without brushing against him, but the blockhead didn't move out of her way like he had for everyone else. *Was he experiencing the same thing?* And if he was, why was he able to hold it together so much better than her?

As she squeezed herself past him, holding in her breath to avoid touching him, he said quietly, "We didn't get to introduce ourselves properly outside—"

"I'm Edon," the Beta chimed in, winking at her, making her smile.

Zelda wanted to make a crack about the Beta speaking before the Alpha but contained herself. No need to bite the hand that was about to feed her and her Pack.

"I'm Dylan." She detected an edge to his tone.

She turned her gaze back to him. Maybe he wasn't so kind after all. It was hard to get a read on him, and that bugged her. She had always been able to peg someone's true nature very quickly. Why couldn't she do the same for her own Mate? "Zelda."

"Named for—"

Not this again. "If you say the video game, I swear—"

"I was going to say Fitzgerald."

That was a first. No one ever figured that out. "Yes. My mother was a fan. She got to name me since my father insisted they name my older brother after her." She slammed her mouth shut. Why had she shared all of that?

He smiled and her stomach flipped. "Nice to meet you."

Zelda didn't return the sentiment. Her body might have made up its mind, but she wasn't sure she agreed with it. When he started walking beside her to the front of the room, she bit her tongue. It wasn't his fault that his body heat was putting her on edge. Scratch that. From the small smile he wore, he knew what he was doing, which meant it most definitely *was* his fault. Why did she like him so much when his behavior kept flipping from a genuine nice guy to toxic masculinity? Contrary to popular belief, not all male werewolves were hyped up on testosterone and domineering.

Dylan's Beta placed two fingers in his mouth whistled loudly. All the wolves from both their Packs stopped talking amongst themselves and paid attention to the two of them.

Furniture had been moved to the edges of the room, but it still didn't explain how the unassuming house fit the forty-odd wolves in the living room alone. From the outside, it looked like it could be one of those small house hotels with maybe four bedrooms. But to hold so many people in the common spaces was still a surprise. The walls and floor were wood and it looked more like what someone would see in a magazine advertising a rustic getaway than a normal home. The strong smell of chili filled the kitchen and she had no doubt that the Morsure Pack would devour it in moments if they were like every other group of werewolves. The question was if there would be enough to feed her Pack, too.

"Welcome, everyone," Dylan started. "As I told your Alpha when we met in the clearing, I am happy to host you all until we can come to a more definitive way to help you. When not in wolf form, Pack matters can only be discussed in human form when on our property. Aside from those locations, and specifically in town, we keep it human-friendly only to avoid detection. Our territory goes from where our Packs met to the lake. Please never go out in wolf form alone. We have a human hunting problem in the Bayou and no one wants to end up with a bullet in their side—or worse."

His voice became low and somehow dangerous at the end and she wondered if he had experienced a personal loss like she had. She made a mental note to ask him if they stuck around long enough to have a personal conversation. What was she saying? Of course, she wouldn't be staying after he'd helped her. Being around him made her even more unsure of herself—and that was the last thing she needed.

He turned toward her, and she took the cue to say her piece. "Thank you for taking us in. I apologize for our abrupt and unexpected arrival. I promise the Equinox Pack will respect the rules laid out and will behave as respectful guests during our temporary stay." She turned to look out at their audience, leveling her gaze at Raoul when she reached him. She heard him curse under his breath. Which meant Dylan had, too. She forced herself to sound pleasant and not pissed off like she really felt. "That will be all for now."

Edon quickly began directing her Pack to a different building separate from both the main house and gym. He was so upbeat and positive that she could easily imagine him working at a college during welcome week, or even being a fraternity boy during recruitment. She would know. But he seemed a lot nicer than that lot, so maybe that wasn't the right comparison. She started to follow him when Dylan said, "You can stay in my room."

She stared at him. Was he crazy? "And why would I do that?"

He met her gaze with an impenetrable one of his own. She saw his easy-going demeanor disappear. God help her, she was attracted to this side of him. "Because you're my Mate and you know it."

Zelda felt goosebumps rise on her skin. "I'm staying with my Pack." She forced the words out quickly, hoping her voice didn't wobble. "They need me nearby."

"And you will be. Besides, they'll have their Beta with them."

Why was he being so obstinate? Strike that. She knew why. "I'm not sleeping with you."

He smiled. "Now, you're being a bit presumptuous. And you never did tell me your Pack's title."

"Equinox. And I don't think I am. *You* told me to sleep in your room and used our being Mates as the reason. What was I supposed to think other than that you wanted to complete the Ritual?"

He reached up and rubbed the back of his head. "Fair enough."

She tried to ignore his arm and chest muscles but failed spectacularly. And she hadn't been expecting him to admit she was right. "So, it's settled. I'm staying with my Pack." She began to walk away, but he stopped her in her tracks with his one-word response.

"No."

She took a deep breath and squashed her desire to punch him. She turned around but didn't close the distance she'd put between them. "I'm not debating this with you. I don't tell you how to run your Pack, you don't get to make decisions about how I run mine."

"I could give you the guest room." She could tell how much he didn't want to say that, but he was clearly desperate. She wondered why. "Tell me why you're refusing to stay in the main house with me, and I'll consider letting you stay in the other house."

"No one *lets* me do anything. I'm an Alpha like you. And if you think—" Zelda cut herself off. As much as she wanted to point out how grotesquely sexist he was acting, the truth remained that her Pack still needed his help. Alienating, or worse, pissing him off, would do nothing but make things harder for her.

He didn't seem offended, though. The only reaction she could see was his left eyebrow ticked a notch higher than his right.

"Because I don't know you, your Pack probably doesn't want a stranger bunking in the main house with them, and I don't believe in receiving better treatment than my Pack members." It was true, but they both knew those weren't the only reasons.

He stared at her for a few moments, and she fought the urge to fidget under his close scrutiny. She was so anxious she felt as if she was back in middle school. When she was about to lose her mind, he finally said, "Okay. It's on the right once you've walked through the front door. You can find the gym through the kitchen door. It has almost everything you need to blow off steam."

Did she imagine him lowering his voice at the end of that statement? His facial expression didn't reflect the smugness she expected, so maybe she had imagined it.

"Thank you," she managed. "And don't tell anyone we're Mates." It was an impulsive but necessary thing to say. If anyone found out about their connection, the chance to prove herself as Alpha would disappear, and she'd be stuck in te shadow of yet another man. Dylan wasn't Liekos, but she sure as hell wasn't going to become a Luna, the glorified trophy wife of an Alpha. He knew nothing about her Pack, and just because he was male didn't mean he would lead them better than her.

His mouth dropped open, but he recovered quickly. Then he opened his mouth again and she knew she was in for it.

Without giving him a chance to argue about yet another thing, she walked away. She didn't need anyone—least of all *him*—to know she was running away with her tail tucked between her legs.

CHAPTER 3

DYLAN WATCHED EDON WALK BACK IN, PASSING ZELDA as he did. She said something to him. Dylan extended his hearing to listen in, but they stopped talking before he could catch anything. She left without a backward glance at him, and Dylan noticed Edon admiring her. A tight band of fury settled around his chest and he growled low.

His Beta's gaze snapped to his and understanding dawned on his face. "You've got to be kidding me."

"I'm not."

"When did you know?"

"When I saw her in human form before the joint meeting."

"So, you dump your girlfriend and find your Mate? That's crazy timing. Can you imagine if you met yesterday? *That* would have been bad." His friend smiled, so Dylan knew he was half-joking.

He'd never said it out loud, nor had anyone else, but there had been times when he wondered if his Mate even existed. Neither of them had gone looking for each other, but they had come together all the same. Why on earth it did, though, was still a mystery.

Dylan glanced at the ceiling.

And why hadn't he felt their Bond in the clearing? He briefly wondered if somehow she *wasn't* his Mate. True, not all Supernaturals immediately realized who their soulmate was upon meeting, but werewolves were supposed to be different.

But what if it was instead some magic, concealment trick like what happened with Fawn and Caleb? The Council had never shared an instance of something similar happening to werewolves, but if it could happen to an angel and the most powerful witch on earth, wasn't anything possible? And he'd never heard of a traceless Mate suddenly appearing. Once they had transformed back into human form, his reaction was what he'd always imagined it. The instant recognition of your perfect half every young wolf looked forward to finding.

As happy as he was to have found her, he still felt uneasy about it.

Edon cleared his throat and Dylan realized he'd been silent for too long. "I have absolutely no idea," he answered.

"Wait until your father and the Pack hear about this! We can finally stop pretending your position is temporary and make it official that you're the new Alpha."

His gaze snapped back to his best friend's. "Let's not push my father into early retirement just yet. You can't tell anyone else, Edon. At least, not yet."

Edon's excited smile shattered and Dylan felt like a jerk who just popped a kid's birthday balloon. But he couldn't do anything else. What type of Mate would he be if the first thing he did was ignore a request that meant a lot to Zelda? *The same kind as Zelda, who had picked sleeping near her Beta over her Mate.* He rejected the thought. She wanted to be near her Pack. It was different. Maybe if he kept telling himself that, he'd believe it.

"Why not?"

"She doesn't want anyone knowing." And it kind of killed him to think of himself as her dirty little secret.

"And you're okay with that?"

Hell no. It was not only a strange request but a ridiculous one. Who wanted to hide the amazing news of finding their Mate? Had she not looked ready to take his head off earlier, he would have asked her just that. "I'm trying to not piss her off further until we've had more time to talk about our relationship and everything else."

"I don't get what's left to discuss. Your relationship should be a done deal. You both know you're each other's Mate. End of story."

"There's more for us to talk about than just that. We're both Alphas. Our Packs would have to merge. That will require a lot of work. And the Beta hates me, although I don't know why." It was rare for a Beta to be more aggressive than their Alpha.

Edon nodded, not bothering to deny the truth of his assessment. "Do you know why they're here yet?"

"Not yet." It hadn't exactly been at the forefront of his mind once he had gotten her alone. And he knew that he'd have to learn the reason for their sudden arrival and why she didn't want people knowing about them. Usually, Mates being united were immediately announced to the Packs involved and celebrated. The fact that she wanted to avoid it made him uneasy. But he wasn't going to judge her until he knew the whole story. And once he did, he'd figure out what to do next. There was no use in making plans with now information to work off. He just hoped she'd be a little more forthcoming so he could help her.

"She doen't look too happy with you."

Dylan cleared his throat. He seemed to be having that effect on all the she-wolves he was talking to today. "I may have unwisely demanded that she stay with me in my room."

Edon whistled, making it very clear how badly he'd messed up, but wisely stayed quiet on the subject.

"I also offered the guest room," he added, feeling like he had to defend himself. "I don't like how close her Beta seems to be with her."

"He's her Beta. It's no different than the two of us."

Dylan wasn't so sure. Yes, he had accidentally disrespected the guy's Alpha, but his reaction was more territorial than Dylan had ever seen Edon or Edon's dad Connor get when defending their Pack. It seemed more *personal* to the Equinox Beta, and it bothered Dylan. He wasn't sure if it was jealousy, but it was an unpleasant feeling all the same. One he wanted to rid himself of as soon as possible. He just had to avoid thinking of the two of them alone in the extra house. With the rest of their Pack, he reminded himself.

"Please extend an invitation for dinner to Alpha Makris and her Beta. I'm sure it'll be better received coming from you. We'll go to

Bourbon Street, and the Packs can eat here. We have enough food for tonight because I made extra, but tomorrow we'll need to stock up now that we have more mouths to feed."

Edon nodded. "I'll leave Max in charge while we're gone. Should I make a reservation somewhere?"

"I will at Café DuMonde. Everyone new to New Orleans should go. Tell them it'll be casual. I'm sure they don't have anything fancy with them, but it'll probably make them feel less self-conscious."

Edon was already walking out the door by the time he finished speaking. Which was ironic since his Beta would have called that an act of insubordination from anyone else in their Pack.

Dylan pulled out his cellphone and debated on telling Fawn immediately that he'd found his soulmate. He even went as far as pulling up their text conversation before he decided against it and locked his screen. She'd have too many questions he was woefully unprepared to answer. And he'd tell his father about it once he'd squared things up with Zelda. Better to have things settled between them before he told anyone about their connection.

But he knew that living in such close quarters would make it difficult to keep private. Packs were known for gossiping, and two of them made secrets nearly impossible.

ZELDA WAS FUMING AS SHE WALKED THE FIFTY steps from the front door to the additional lodge. How dare he demand she stay in the same room as him? Not if he was the last man—human, werewolf, or something else—alive and his shelter was the last one in existence.

She passed her Pack members whose eyes all darted toward a closed door in the back. Probably her and Raoul's room.

She opened the door and saw him pacing like a caged, pissed-off animal, despite the generous size of the room. She could relate.

"I don't like him," her Beta declared before the door had even closed behind her.

Raoul should have at least waited until they had privacy. What if someone from the Morsure Pack heard him insulting their Alpha? Who was also her Mate. She suppressed the shudder that moved through her body, a slightly calmer version of her first reaction to him. It still was enough to make her heart pound in her ears.

Zelda closed her eyes and shoved her personal feelings into a mental box. They wouldn't be helpful for the upcoming conversation because she honestly agreed more with her best friend than with what she was about to say. "You don't have to," she said with a sigh, "but you can't keep toeing the line of antagonizing Dylan. He's the Alpha of a bigger Pack than ours, and he's being very hospitable to us. You have to let it go."

"If anyone else had done the same thing, you would have been growling even more than me, reminding everyone just who the Alpha was. You don't take crap from anyone. But around him? It's like you've turned into some simpering puppy."

Before she could respond, there was a knock at their door. "Who is it?" she called.

"Edon."

Had he overheard them? She pointed at Raoul, "This discussion isn't over. Once he's gone, you're going to apologize to Alpha Stone."

Her Beta didn't respond, but he at least he didn't argue.

She opened the door and saw the Morsure Pack's Beta. "Yes?"

Edon's eyebrows had nearly disappeared into his hair when he saw both of them in the room. He didn't comment, but she would bet everything she had, which admittedly wasn't much at the moment, that Dylan would be hearing about her sleeping arrangements before the night was over. She mentally braced herself for *that* confrontation.

"Alpha Makris wanted to extend a dinner invitation to you and your Beta tonight. We'll be leaving for the Quarter in thirty minutes. You can meet us in front of the main house since we'll be taking the truck." He turned and left before she could even respond.

Raoul growled behind her. "He's already ordering us around like his Pack members?"

Zelda closed the door. "He invited us to dinner, so keep the claws in. I'm trying to keep a level head tonight and I don't need you making that harder for me."

"You saying that tells me you don't have one."

"Are you questioning my ability to be an effective Alpha? Because that's low, Raoul. Really low."

Now he sighed. "I'm sorry. That was a cheap shot and not at all fair. I'm just pissed. We're not his to order around. *You're* my Alpha. He needs to remember that."

"I'll remind him at dinner."

DYLAN WATCHED FROM HIS BEDROOM WINDOW AS ZELDA and her Beta walked toward his truck. He opened his door before Edon had the chance to knock.

His best friend cleared his throat. "Just so you know, they're sharing a room."

His vision went completely red—which had only happened a few times before. The last time had been a few years ago when he had seen a group of demons attacking Fawn when he was helping her fight Lucifer's forces in Central Park.

Edon quickly backed up. "Wanted to give you a head's up before you smelled him on her."

"Edon," he growled. "Stop. Talking. Now."

"I heard the tail end of a conversation. I don't think they're involved that way. They sounded just like a normal Alpha and Beta."

He glared at his friend. "What did I just say?"

Don't kill him, all right? Your Mate would probably kill you.

He didn't need the reminder. And hearing Edon's voice in his head right now just gave his own chaotic thoughts even less space. He was going to get a headache before the night was over.

Aside from Mates, only Alphas and their Betas had that ability in human form. He was grateful for that. He loved his Pack, but if they all had a direct line to his mind all the time, even a one-way connection, he'd go crazy.

Dylan took a deep breath. "Let's get this dinner over with. And keep your snarkiness to a minimum. We're trying to make a good impression." He made a beeline for the driver's seat. "Zelda, you can take shotgun," he said, ignoring Edon's indignant huff.

He knew Edon wasn't actually upset.

Dylan glanced at his Mate as she climbed into the car. He forced himself to look away from her deep green summer dress and how nice it complemented her.

Sitting this close to her, he could smell her Beta on her. His hands tightened on the wheel.

They reached the restaurant and met the hostess out front. "Hey, Viv. Four for dinner?"

"Right this way." She smiled at him and grabbed four menus. "It's been a while. I can't even remember the last time you were here." She glanced over at Zelda and her Beta. "And you brought friends?"

If only she knew the truth. "They're just passing through for a bit. Wanted them to experience the magic here."

"It is a rite of passage, after all." She paused, eyeing him thoughtfully. "You're still with that Bailey chick, right?"

He shook his head and she smiled.

"Thank God," Viv said. "She was such a thorn in your side."

"She's still around though."

"That's a shame." Viv touched his arm in sympathy.

Zelda cleared her throat and he looked back at her. Her lips were pressed together in a thin line. She silently sat in her chair, her Beta across from her.

He saw Edon shaking his head.

This was going to be a long dinner.

CHAPTER 4

ZELDA LIFTED THE MENU AND BLANKLY STARED AT it. She tried to focus, but she was too distracted by the anger that was currently
electrifying her nerve endings. She barely held in the growl building
in her chest.

Their waitress, *Viv*, as Dylan fondly called her, was blatantly flirt-
ing with her Mate. And he wasn't doing anything to reject her advanc-
es. What happened to his devotion to the sanctity of the Mate bond?
Was she an ex? She hated the jealousy that clouded her mind, but she
couldn't seem to get rid of it.

Raoul, who was seated opposite her and next to the subject of her
problems, raised his eyebrow at her in silent challenge. *Still want me
on my best behavior?*

Yes. She hadn't yet told him that she and Alpha Stone were Mates.
She wasn't sure she wanted to tell him *at all*, which was beyond unrealistic. He was her Beta, and that revelation affected him. He'd lose his
position once everyone knew she was Dylan's Mate.

Although female Alphas were no longer outlawed, they were still
rare. And when a female Alpha found her Mate, if the Mate was male,
it was an unspoken rule that his Pack would absorb hers. And right
now? That would be disastrous. She was still settling into the leader
position and she'd be damned if she handed it over just because she
had coincidentally found her Mate.

Zelda heard Dylan clear his throat and her gaze cut to his. Viv had disappeared and she was glad for it. She watched his Adam's apple bob and knew that he could see her anger. Good. She just hoped neither of their Betas figured out what was happening.

Out of the corner of her eye, she realized that maybe she was a little late in preventing that. It seemed Edon had been let in on the secret because, despite his blank expression, he sat too attentively to be ignorant of the situation.

The waiter came over, and thankfully, it was a short interaction. After taking their food order he asked, "Would you like anything to drink?"

Did she ever. Maybe it would take the edge off and they'd be able to get through the meal without causing a scene. Because now that she looked at Dylan, he seemed tense, too. How had she missed that before? "Can you make a Moscow Mule?"

"Can I see some ID?"

She reached into her back pocket and handed it over.

He checked it and said, "Coming right up."

"Is there a specific reason you invited us to dinner?" She kept her voice light when she wanted to shake Dylan for bringing them to this restaurant where someone had a crush on him. He couldn't be *that* dense, could he?

Dylan took a sip of his water. "You still haven't told me why the Equinox Pack needs our help. I thought it would be a good idea to have the conversation as soon as possible so I know what I'm dealing with. I can't help if I don't know what you need."

"We lost our territory in a land dispute with another Pack."

Her Mate frowned.

"It wasn't my idea," she quickly added. She didn't want him thinking she was inept or unstable. "My brother was stupid to think it would ever work. The other Pack retaliated and killed him and his Beta, who was Raoul's older brother."

"I'm sorry to hear you both lost your brothers. Mourning them must have been difficult while you were adjusting to your new positions. And it's nice to officially meet you, Raoul."

Her Beta just nodded and she kicked him lightly under the table.

"Likewise," he muttered.

Dylan didn't say anything, but she could have sworn she saw his emerald eyes briefly flash with irritation.

Luckily, the waiter came back with their drinks before the animosity emanating between the men could escalate. "Are you ready to order? Sorry for the wait, it's been a busy night."

"It always is," Edon said, speaking for the first time since they had all come together for dinner. From the short conversations she'd had with him, he seemed like a nice person. She looked forward to learning more about him, but from the way Dylan was watching her, she wasn't sure she'd have much of an opportunity. Her Mate was clearly a possessive one, but he wasn't about to control her every move. He might be her Mate, but he wasn't her Alpha.

D YLAN GLARED AT HIS BETA, WHO WAS SITTING across the table from him with a smug smile. *You're treading on thin ice.* Edon raised an eyebrow at him, and if they weren't in public and around humans, he would have called him out disrespecting his Alpha.

He knew it was an overreaction, but it seemed he couldn't keep his cool when it came to Zelda. And the idea that she liked his Beta more than him rankled. But he knew it wasn't their fault. He had come on very strong. Even so, was it normal for a Mate to have to work so hard for the other to like him? Or was Zelda particularly stubborn, like all the other women in his life?

I'm just being nice, Edon teased.

"So," Zelda said, "you're pretty young to be an Alpha..."

"I'm filling in for my father while he's away." That was the official answer, but he had the sneaking suspicion that his stepping into the leadership role was a final test more than a temporary stint like he'd been telling people.

His dad had been gone for three weeks, off who knew where. Dylan had only found out he was leaving the morning of his departure. The day after, Connor left to join Marcus, and they hadn't heard from either of them ever since. Dylan wondered if they were tracking someone. But if they were, they wouldn't have left the Pack behind, no matter how much faith they had in him and Edon.

"Why isn't your father's Beta in charge?" Raoul asked.

Dylan turned his attention to him, but Edon spoke first. "My father is Alpha Stone's companion. As neither of them is here right now, as their sons, we have to step in until they return."

Zelda's gaze hadn't left him even as his friend spoke. Her eyes narrowed and her head tilted slightly to the side as if she were looking at him in a new light. He wasn't sure if that was a good or bad.

"It must be nice to have your father around," she finally said, a hint of sadness in her tone.

"When did yours pass away?" he asked, reading between the lines.

"Last year. The worst part was that it was so sudden. He was alive... and then he wasn't." She paused. "I thought I'd have him for a lot longer."

She seemed so small all of a sudden. Right now, all he wanted to do was to hold her. As if she had heard his private wish, her posture stiffened and she squared her shoulders in an obvious move to mask how she felt. He wondered how often she had to do that since her father's death. Being the Alpha meant having a lot of freedom, but it also meant having less privacy. The Pack was almost always looking to you for guidance, and no wolf wanted to follow someone they considered weak. Normally, he never felt the strain, but since meeting Zelda, he could empathize with wanting to let it all out and knowing he couldn't.

He knew that he hadn't replied to her last statement, but he felt that all he could possibly say would either be tone-deaf, not enough, or cliché. Had he known his Mate better, he would have known exactly how to comfort her. "I know the feeling," he finally said.

The beignets arrived, and he handed his credit card over. As some of the restaurant's best customers, Viv was usually the one to bring his dessert over, but he was thankful she had sent their waiter instead. Zelda had looked like she wanted to claw the hostess' eyes out earlier. It was best that Vivienne was out of striking distance. Edon might have thought he didn't notice before, but he wasn't *that* unobservant. And a little part of him was pleased to know that she felt even a modicum of possessiveness toward him because he felt his control slipping when it came to her.

Z ELDA STARED AT THE STOPLIGHTS, WATCHING THEM TURN from red to green until her eyes started to water from the lack of blinking.

Dylan had understood her losing her father more than empty sympathy. He'd only mentioned his father in passing, and she wondered if he'd lost his mother to a hunter. When he warned her Pack of human hunters, he didn't sound just sad but also had an edge. Like he had never gotten closure.

She sank in her seat and tried to resist the urge to comfort him.

When they got back, Dylan killed the ignition, but he didn't climb out. He merely sat there, watching the house.

She could see shadows of people moving on the first floor. The top floor was dark. She wondered what was up there. Bedrooms, she assumed, since she couldn't find any on the first floor.

Edon opened his door and immediately stepped out. "I'm going to make sure the house isn't a mess."

Zelda wasn't sure if that was an excuse. When they'd unexpectedly arrived, the house seemed to be in order despite the number of wolves in the Morsure Pack.

Raoul waited in the car.

Make sure our Pack helps clean up.

In the rearview mirror, she saw her Beta glance at Dylan before he climbed out and walked toward the main house.

Her Mate didn't even flinch when the truck door slammed. "He doesn't like me much, does he?"

"He'll get over it." She'd make sure of it. She might have her issues with Dylan, but they were both Alphas and Mates. On the same level in every way, whereas Raoul was disrespecting another Alpha.

"He doesn't know."

It wasn't a question, but she answered, anyway. "But your Beta does. Can he be discreet?"

"Edon can take a secret to his grave without anyone knowing he's keeping one to begin with."

"Good." She opened the door, pausing when Dylan spoke.

"Can we talk before you go back to the guest house?"

She crossed her arms. "About what?" *Don't encourage him*, she scolded herself. She pushed open the car door and stepped out. Being alone with him was dangerous for her self-control. If she ran, would she reach the house before him?

She hadn't come up with an answer before Dylan got out of the truck and locked it. He glanced at her over the hood of the car. "You. Me. As individuals, not Alphas."

She didn't answer. Instead, she walked toward the house and he kept in step with her. Before they reached the door, she heard a stampede of footsteps. Soon after, Edon and Raoul reappeared.

"That was fast," she said.

"I told them that whoever cleaned up the most would automatically be eliminated from the laundry pool." The Beta shifted his glance to Dylan, then back to her. "Well, now that that's settled, I'm going to sleep." He started walking up the stairs to the second floor. Leaping might have been more accurate since he was taking them two at a time. She'd never seen someone so excited to sleep in her life.

Her Mate rolled his eyes. "Say hi to Anna for me. And tell her to hang out with everyone more. I'm sure your mom can handle herself for a few minutes."

Edon tossed one last remark over his shoulder. "Tell her yourself and see how that works out for you." The door closed and she heard his footsteps climbing more stairs inside.

Raoul cleared his throat and she focused on him. "If our work is done here—" He started walking toward the door, his hand hovering over the handle as he sent an expectant look toward her.

"It's not," Dylan cut in. "I still need to speak to Zelda about some logistics. It won't take long."

The hell he does, she heard Raoul snarl in her mind.

"I'll see you later," she said, her tone firm. She didn't have the time or the energy to referee a pissing contest between the two men.

Her Beta forced a nod and walked stiffly back to the second house where their Pack waited for them.

To Dylan's benefit, he didn't gloat. He merely walked to the door and held it open for her. She walked past him into the house. *I hope I don't regret this.*

D YLAN OPENED THE LIQUOR CABINET. HIS FATHER AND Connor had been building the collection since before either he or Edon were born. There were a lot of bottles to choose from. "Pick your poison."

His Mate didn't look before answering, "Vodka neat." He heard her situating herself on one of the bar stools at the marble countertop and glanced at her over his shoulder. "Should I be concerned?"

She leveled a glare at him.

He took the hint and didn't bother to explain that it had been a joke. He grabbed two shot glasses and set them down in front of her. He poured hers until it was to overflowing when she never told him to stop. He poured the other to match. He pushed hers across the counter and held his up. "Cheers."

Surprisingly, she met his glass with her own. He tossed his shot back and poured himself another. He walked around the counter, ignoring her wary gaze that tracked his movements as he sat next to her.

She finished her shot in one go, then placed the empty glass on the counter. He pointed to the bottle, but she shook her head. "Were you lying to Raoul just now?"

"You still haven't told me what you expect me to do for your Pack." Would she bring up the obvious solution?

"You said you wanted to get to know me better?" she asked, changing the subject. "What do you want to know?"

He propped his head on his hand and turned toward her. He didn't lean any closer, though. He made sure to keep the distance between them she wanted to preserve. "You told me a little about your father. But I want to know the whole story. And what about your mom?"

"My dad got caught in a bear trap and was shot by a hunter. My brother is the one who found him." Her words were clipped and coming out quickly. "My mom died in a fire years ago. Dad couldn't get to her in time after he saved me and my brother." He could see tears threatening to spill and quickly handed her a tissue.

She took it wordlessly. A few moments passed before she composed herself again. "What about your mom?"

Dylan turned the full shot glass between his hands. "Also killed by a hunter." He swallowed the angry lump in his throat that never failed to appear when he remembered what happened. "Who is a friend of my father. He has no idea we're werewolves, or that he killed my mom. He just thinks that my mom suddenly died from an aneurysm. The worst part is that he was poaching on our territory at the time."

"What did your dad do?"

He drank his second shot and slammed the empty glass on the table. "My dad called the Pack off from attacking him."

Zelda stood on the rung of the stool and leaned over the marble to reach for the bottle. She grabbed it and poured herself a second.

"I don't want to end tonight on a downer," he said. "So, tell me something about yourself." When she didn't volunteer anything, he added, "What's your favorite thing to do?"

"Martial arts."

Dylan ignored the enticing image of her working out. "Get in a lot of fights, did you?"

Zelda leaned in until he could practically taste the alcohol on her lips. He swallowed and forced himself to stay still instead of giving in to his instinct to close the remaining distance and kiss her.

"That's for me to know, and for you to..."

"Find out?" he supplied.

She puffed out a silent laugh but refused to answer. Instead, she pushed back from the counter. She picked up her shot glass, walked around him to place it in the sink, and walked to the back door.

He just stood watching her retreating figure.

She glanced at him over her shoulder. "Goodnight, Dylan."

"Goodnight, Zelda."

He stared at the wooden door long it shut behind her.

CHAPTER 5

Z ELDA SLIPPED INTO THE BACK BUILDING. HER PACK'S snores filled the hallway. She silently cracked open the door to the room she was sharing with Raoul and found him already lying down. He'd taken up the whole bed and was facing the wall. She closed the door and reached behind her neck. She was halfway through unzipping her dress when she heard the mattress shift under him.

She paused, afraid to turn around. Was he awake? Watching her?

Who cared if he was? she scolded herself. They'd seen each other change often enough. Aside from being Alpha and Beta, being close friends meant they had very few personal boundaries.

She forced her hand to continue until the zipper stopped at the base of her back. Holding the front of the dress to her chest, she leaned over her backpack and pulled out her pajamas. She let the dress drop and heard a sharp intake of breath, confirming her earlier suspicion.

Shit.

Zelda only changed in the room instead of the bathroom because she thought he was sleeping. Obviously, she'd been wrong. She pulled her top and stepped into the shorts before turning around.

Raoul was now facing her. Staring, to be more precise.

She waited for him to say something, but she wasn't sure she wanted to hear anything he had to say.

"That was fast," he finally said after an uncomfortable silence.

She forced herself to relax. "Dylan said it wouldn't take long."

Raoul frowned and she wanted to smack herself for bringing him up. No need to antagonize her Beta right before sleep.

She faked a yawn and then found herself really yawning. "I'm tired."

He stood and let her settle on the side closest to the wall. She wasted no time pulling the covers over herself and turning away from her best friend. She couldn't get the sound of his surprised gasp out of her head. Were things changing between them? Zelda knew humans who had met them always assumed they'd get together. She'd even heard some of their Pack members whispering about it, but always with the caveat of "if they were Mates," which they weren't. And she'd never seen him as anything more than a best friend.

But if his feelings about her were shifting from platonic to romantic, the universe had really shitty timing.

She shut her eyes even tighter and willed the thoughts to go away. Raoul was her best friend, nothing more.

The next morning, Zelda followed her Pack with Raoul by her side as they all made their way to the main house for breakfast. He made no mention of the night before, and for that she was grateful. She'd be happy to never think of it again but doubted that would be possible.

She saw Dylan in the middle of the kitchen, personally handing out plates of food to his Pack members. If he noticed her, he didn't show it. Didn't even glance her way.

Edon, on the other hand, sauntered right over. "Good morning! Want me to make you two plates?"

"We can do it ourselves," Raoul grumbled.

"No thank you," she amended with a smile. What the hell was Raoul's problem? After last night, she thought he understood that his behavior was unacceptable, but it seemed her words had had no impact on him. She frowned. That had never happened before. Normally, he would hear her side not just because she was his Alpha, but also because they were friends and that's what friends did.

As they waited in line, she turned her thoughts to the other difficult and confusing male in her life. Yesterday, he seemed to be hovering all the time. And yet now he almost acted as if she wasn't there at all.

She needed to snap out of it. Who cared how much attention he was paying her? She didn't even want him to announce they were Mates, and his undivided attention would be sure to raise unwanted questions. No. Things were better as they were. She just needed things to be normal. Dylan could ignore her and Raoul could get back to being the laid back guy she'd known her whole life.

She ate her food in silence and went up to get seconds. Whenever she was among humans, she stuck to one serving—stupid societal expectations on women, and all—but among fellow werewolves, she knew she wouldn't be judged. They all knew that their bodies had faster metabolism than most species, including other Supernaturals.

On her way to the buffet table, which Dylan seemed to have some point vacated, another she-wolf hip-checked her. "Excuse me."

The other girl took one glance at her and gave her a look that left her skin prickling. "So, you're the one he's chasing now. Yeah, I heard you leaving last night," she added before Zelda could reply. "It won't last long. He's not cut out for relationships. Fawn really broke his heart. Not even I could get him to move on."

Then you'll know nothing happened. "And you are?" Zelda bit out, surprisingly able to keep from growling.

"Bailey. Dylan's ex."

Wasn't that just fantastic? "Excuse me." She sidestepped her new acquaintance and filled her plate with less food than she had originally intended. Her appetite was gone.

"Bailey, I thought I told everyone to be nice to our guests. And I remember seeing you in the room where I made the announcement."

Zelda's spine straightened when she heard Dylan's voice behind her. When had he come so close?

"Yes, *Alpha*," was her reply.

Zelda took her plate and walked back to the table as fast as possible while also avoiding attention.

"You okay?" Raoul asked. "You look pale."

"I'm okay."

"Ignore Bailey," Edon chimed in. "She can be a pain in the ass. She thrives on drama."

YLAN HAD HEARD BAILEY'S CATTY COMMENTS FROM ACROSS the common space. She'd treated Fawn similarly, but his need to protect Zelda against his ex was stronger than what he'd felt in the Belgrave apartment a few years ago, back when his first love had been struggling with her own soulmate.

"I'll ask you again. *Why* do you keep her around?"

He tossed Edon a rag and bottle of cleaning spray. "Because I'm not going to toss her out just because we don't see eye to eye." He quickly wiped down the table where his Mate had sat only an hour ago. Right after the meal, she'd disappeared with Raoul. He tried not to think about it. Giving her space had been hard but based on the number of times he felt her gaze on him throughout the morning, it had been the right choice.

"Doesn't mean she doesn't deserve it."

He shot his best friend a disapproving look. "That's not what a good Alpha would do. Why are you so hung up on this, anyway? You've had it out for her ever since I started dating her."

Edon snorted. "Yeah, well, if we want to talk about good behavior, she's never fit the bill. Cassidy always said she was mean, and my sister wasn't wrong. Why you insist on being the bigger person goes beyond me." He tossed the bottle back and Dylan caught it mid-air.

They kept moving through the tables in pairs until they were all clean. How the four picnic tables fit into the main area of the home still confused him, but he assumed it had to do with the same spell Stella Belgrave had cast on her New York apartment. Expanding it so it was bigger on the inside.

Now that he thought about it, the size would probably have to increase even more once Zelda's Pack merged with his. But who knew when that would be? For all he knew, she planned on dragging out their Mate status being a secret for a month. He refused to consider her demanding an even longer timetable. That would be crazy. No matter what, he'd have to ask his dad about that when the time came.

In the meantime, he had other matters at hand. "Hey, do you know where your dad is?"

"No idea. Why?"

"Need to ask him something." Alphas and Betas were connected via a mental connection so strong that it only came second to the one that existed between Mates. Since Connor was his dad's Beta, he could only contact him psychically if he was nearby. Which meant he needed the man to have access to a cellphone right now. "Do you think he's in human form right now?"

"It's still early, so maybe. Apart from Pack business, he always likes Shifting after sundown. Can I ask why you're talking to him instead of your dad?"

"Don't want to bring him in too early. I want to handle this on my own if I can."

Edon didn't bother hiding his skepticism. "Right..."

"Shut up. You know what I mean. I don't want to involve my dad unless I have to. He's testing me to see if I'm ready to lead. If I called him before I even had a plan, how would that look?"

"You don't know that for certain. Yes, this is a trial run, but did you see your dad before he left? He needed a break. And he obviously trusts you to keep things running, but he's not going to penalize you for having a question. You still have to find a Mate—well, *he* thinks you still have to find her. He's not going to make you Alpha without that being official, so why not ask him for help?"

"What else do you call my father leaving the state for an indefinite period beside early retirement?"

"A long-overdue vacation? Didn't I just explain that, or was that all in my head? You know, Anna hates when I have a whole conversation by myself—"

"Don't be smart."

"Can't help it," Edon quipped, tossing the bottle up and catching it behind his back with his other hand. Show off. "Anyway, what's your backup plan if you can't reach my dad?"

Dylan sighed. "I guess I'll ask your mom, then." His dad was still a last resort. One that he hoped he wouldn't have to rely on. Edon probably thought he was being stubborn and prideful. And maybe he was, but this was as much about proving himself to his dad as it was proving to himself that he could handle the responsibilities of being

Alpha. He'd been training his whole life for it, but there were still times he wondered if he'd ever truly be ready. And the confusing situation with Zelda was only making him second-guess himself even more.

"Don't tell her that she was your second choice."

"As if. I like being counted among the living." He was joking, but they both knew that Esme was a force to be reckoned with. Even as Connor's Mate, there was nothing Beta about her. Dylan could imagine her leading her own Pack if she ever decided to, and he wouldn't begrudge her if she did. It would never happen, though. She was too loyal to the Morsure Pack to ever strike out on her own. He punched in Connor's phone number and waited. When it rang out and reached the voicemail prompt, he hung up. "Your mom, it is, then."

Edon snickered.

Dylan flipped him the finger as he walked upstairs and knocked on the room reserved for his Beta's parents. It was technically the master bedroom on the house's blueprints. After his mom died, Marcus had moved into the room on the opposite side of the hall and insisted Connor and Esme move in there. They'd resisted at first, but his dad had eventually worn them down.

"Esme, you in there?"

"Come on in," her voice sounded through the door.

Dylan opened it and saw her crocheting what looked like another throw blanket. She'd made a habit of giving them to newly Mated couples. His eyes narrowed. Had Edon said something or was this just a coincidence?

She met his gaze. "What can I do for you?" She asked, not bothering to look down at her fingers as they twisted and pulled the yarn.

He leaned against the doorjamb and crossed his arms. "Can't I just come to visit you every so often?"

She smiled. "You *could*, but you never do anymore. You're always running around with Edon. I barely see him more than you." She lowered her voice, conspiratorially adding, "It's because I'm his mother and he can't get away with not visiting me. You, on the other hand are future Alpha. But it would be nice if you came by more often. You know I don't bite."

"Sorry," he mumbled.

"It's fine. I know you and my son are busy most of the time. Which brings me back to my first question. What can I do for you?" She fixed him with her best interrogation stare, both eyebrows raised as she waited for an answer. One that had made him and Edon rat on themselves more than he cared to admit. The woman meant business.

"Well, obviously you know I agreed to help a Pack—"

She made a *tsk*-ing sound. "While it's generous of you, I don't think it was a smart choice. You should know by now that Rogues bring nothing but trouble. And they're not going to be comfortable crammed in that back house for long. Besides, you can't help them longer than for two weeks anyway. Not unless a member of our Pack finds a Mate in theirs. And we know how unlikely that is." She sighed, as if she truly pitied the Equinox wolves. She probably did, but like Connor, the Morsure Pack always came first.

She should have been right. Everyone his age already had found their Mates. Everyone who hadn't paired off yet was too young to have ever felt the pull. The probability of a Rogue finding their Mate was slim to none. And him finding Zelda seemed to be nothing more than a statistical fluke. One that was as complicated now as trying to figure out how it happened in the first place.

"They're not technically Rogues," he hedged. "They're temporarily dislocated."

"Have they told the Council?"

"I have no idea."

"Without their own territory and being officially recognized by the Council, they're Rogues. It's the law. And if they are, they only have a month to find a new home. And it can't be with us unless—"

"One of them has a Mate in our Pack," he finished. "Right," he said, his stomach churning with anxiety. "I guess they'll be relocating soon, then." He hated lying to Esme, but he wasn't sure he was. Until his Mate acknowledged him publicly, he couldn't help her or her Pack. At best, he had a month to convince Zelda to stay. Most likely, he only had half that time. The clock was ticking and he had the sinking feeling it would run out before he was ready.

CHAPTER 6

ZELDA PUT AS MUCH FORCE BEHIND THE HIT as possible without losing her balance. It didn't matter because Raoul dodged, ducking under her arm and landed his elbow between her shoulder blades. She should have seen the move coming, but she'd been distracted, thinking about Dylan instead of her immediate problems. *Again.*

"If that's the best you can do, you must have been cheating that first time we went up against each other."

This was the Raoul she'd been missing. "We both know I can beat your ass any day of the week." They both knew his move had been perfectly within bounds and that a real fight would have no rules at all, but he didn't bring it up like a stuffy instructor might. Her dad definitely would have. And Liekos would have called her a sore loser.

She feigned to the right, then threw a left-handed punch. She smiled when it made a satisfying smack against her best friend's muscle. She didn't let her small victory distract her, though. She took a step forward and landed another quick shot to his side.

When she punched forward again, he went around and trapped her in an arm lock. If they were really enemies, he'd probably have dislocated her shoulder by now. She kicked his shin, but he didn't let go. After three seconds, she tapped his hand and he released her.

He spun her around and held his hand out for her to shake. "I'd say good fight, but—"

She shoved him lightly, knowing it would only express her friendly frustration. "Shut up."

Zelda felt the air change before she heard her Mate. Raoul turned first and growled.

"Can we have a moment?" Dylan called from the entrance. A slight frown tugged at the edges of his mouth. She could also see a faint line between his eyebrows as if he were concentrating on something or contemplating the meaning of life. Maybe he was doing both.

He's always talking to you privately.

He has no other way to communicate with me. It's not like she was about to give him her phone number. Then she'd never get any reprieve. And she really needed to keep distance between them.

Her data plan was already hurting her wallet with all the roaming they'd been doing. She might as well give the cell company her bank password if Dylan's texts started pouring in. Though he wouldn't have to text her at all if she stopped avoiding him and stayed close enough to have normal conversations. She shut that thought down. Neither of those situations was going to happen. Her number would stay private and the distance between her and Dylan would remain intact.

Raoul made a dissatisfied sound before walking away.

Dylan, who had stayed in the threshold the whole time, sidestepped her Beta to let him pass. Only after the door closed, did he come closer to her. "He still doesn't like me."

"I told you to give him time. And he thinks you're taking up too much of mine."

"Didn't realize he had a monopoly on your schedule. Is it his Beta duties that keep him glued to your side or something else?"

She let the comment slide because she wasn't sure how to answer it anymore. Last night she would have known, but now... Maybe she was being unrealistic in expecting the two of them to get along. Despite Raoul being her Beta, he'd always been more aggressive than either his father or brother, acting more like an Alpha with everyone but her. She was the only one he ever let dictate his actions beside himself.

"You know," she finally answered, "it might be more convenient for both of us if you compiled a list of concerns."

"Did you contact the Council when you relocated?"

"No..." How on earth was she supposed to have done that while she and her Pack had been regularly drifting across state borders?

He dragged a hand through his hair. "By law, I can only help you for two weeks. Longer than that and my Pack would get in trouble for harboring Rogues. And as a future Alpha without a Mate, I really can't have another strike against me. The Council has been kind to me, but they can't turn a blind eye if I break one of their laws."

She flinched when he mentioned not having a Mate. She knew what he meant, but it still stung to hear him deny their Bond. Even if it was because he was merely appeasing her by keeping up the pretense she requested. "So that means—?" She cut herself off, unable to form the words. He'd throw her out because the law told him to?

He nodded, answering her unanswered question. "I'm not telling you this because I want to rush you." He took a step back. "Anyway, I just wanted you to know everything you needed to make an informed decision about the next step for your Pack."

Before she could respond, he had walked out of the gym, leaving her alone with the gymnastics mat and the punching bag. Weren't Mates supposed to be loyal to each other no matter what?

When she entered their room, Raoul was waiting for her. "What does he want now?"

"He said we only have two weeks to be here before he can't help us anymore."

"He actually said that?" Raoul jumped to his feet. "I'm going to—"

"It's not his fault," she interrupted, placing a hand on her friend's chest until he sat back down. "We'd all get in trouble."

"I don't know why you care what happens to him," he said, not meeting her gaze. "He's an ass."

"Why don't you like him?" She had her reasons for being conflicted, but she didn't know her best friend's motivation for apparently hating the Morsure Alpha. And his excuse that it was because Dylan had initially assumed she was a Luna could only go so far.

Raoul's eyes flicked from the door to her. "He's arrogant and thinks he's a better leader than either of us. Which is absolute bull to begin with, but we were also thrown into the positions unexpectedly. And now that he knows there's a deadline, who's to say he won't just let the clock run out and toss us back on the streets?"

"He wouldn't do that."

"How would you know? He's a stranger. Anyway, I think the sooner we leave the better."

"I haven't thought of our next step yet."

"Then what have you two been talking about all this time?"

"Ideas. But nothing worth mentioning." *Like us being Mates.* She kept the thought to herself, silently erecting a barrier between her and her Beta. She just hoped he didn't notice.

"Exactly my point. He's not helping." He took her hands in his. "We should just leave now. We ran our Pack fine before ever coming here, we can continue doing that. We don't need his charity. We shouldn't have to depend on his whims to keep a roof over our heads and food in our stomachs. If it makes it any easier, I can get a job, too, wherever we land. So can the others. It shouldn't be all on you."

"We can't make everyone work themselves to the bone. And I'm the Alpha, Raoul. It's my responsibility to carry the Pack."

"I'm not saying they will. But we're a Pack. We're in this together. At least, we should be. But I'm not sure you are right now. You're barely here. You're always with *him.*"

"Of course, I'm in it. But I don't want to make a hasty decision. Let's give it at least a few more days. And be nicer, Raoul. For the sake of everyone." She sat next to him and leaned into him. "You're an amazing guy. Why won't you let the Morsure Pack see that, too?"

"I don't need to impress them."

"It's not about that. Just try... harder. Please?"

His arm came around her shoulder, pulling her closer until her head rested against his. "I will."

She didn't bother to hide the sigh that escaped. "Thank you. And I promise to be more available."

DYLAN WAS WALKING BACK TO THE MAIN HOUSE when he heard a group from the Equinox Pack whispering amongst themselves. He rolled his eyes. Clearly, they weren't being careful about being over-heard. Maybe they had also been eavesdropping and knew that Zelda was currently busy.

"What are we even doing here?" one of them asked. "Have any of you spoken to her since we arrived?"

"How could we? She's never around. Raoul is the only one who's consistently here."

"Do you think she's like her brother?"

There was a pause. "She doesn't *seem* crazy—"

"But neither did he until he became Alpha. Maybe they're set off by stress?"

Dylan couldn't hear anymore and forced himself to walk away. When he entered the kitchen, he found Raoul filling a glass of water. He watched the guy's muscles tense. Clearly, the Beta had heard his approach. Not that he had been trying to sneak up on the guy.

"May I ask a question?" Dylan began.

Raoul shut the sink off and turned around, eyebrow raised in challenge. "Does it matter if I say no?"

"What was Zelda's brother like?"

That seemed to catch him off guard. The Beta took a slow sip then placed the cup near the edge of the counter and crossed his arms over his chest. "In what way?"

"In general, as an Alpha, and so on." He forced his tone to stay light and noncommittal.

"He was kind of like you."

Now it was his turn to be confused. "Explain."

"Liekos always assumed he knew best and told everyone what to do."

Dylan crossed his arms. "Isn't that the job of Alpha?"

"It was his attitude that was the problem. Narcissistic and couldn't stand being wrong." Raoul shrugged. "Got worse when he turned eighteen. But he started acting super irritable and irrationally once he became Alpha. Not even my brother could figure out why." He paused. "Just like I can't tell why you're even asking me about this."

"I heard some of your Pack doubting Zelda's leadership. They called her brother crazy."

"There were rumors."

"Was there any truth to them?"

Raoul chugged the water like it was a lifeline. Then he refilled it and spoke over the running water. "Can't say for sure. But he didn't have a Mate, so there was that."

"Is it affecting Zelda?"

"No. She has me. I've always been there for anything she needs."

He felt the hairs on his neck raise and he swallowed the growl threatening to burst forward at the Beta's insinuation. "Such as?"

Raoul ignored his question. "I can guess why you're asking, though. Any Pack must be worried about a Mate-less Alpha. For your sake, I hope you fare better than her brother."

Dylan doubted the sincerity of his words. It had been a lingering concern for everyone around him. "Thank you. But I've actually found her." But he wasn't feeling the relief he should be at such a discovery.

"Really? Why wasn't she next to you during the welcome speech? Do you hide her in the attic or something?"

Dylan clenched his jaw. He knew Raoul was being an ass on purpose, but it still got under his skin more than he wished it did. "We have some complicated circumstances we're working through first."

"She hate the idea of being stuck with you for life?"

Dylan shook his head. Opening his mouth now wouldn't be helpful.

"What are you, twelve? Making up a girl to sound cooler?"

"No. I respect her choices, so I'm protecting her privacy like she asked me to." Which was the mature thing to do. How on Earth had this guy become the Beta of the Equinox Pack? Not even Edon was this sophomoric.

"Wow. She must be some girl to have you wrapped around her finger already. Or, you're a lot weaker than you pretend to be. Come on, tell me who it is. I can't wait to hear it."

Dylan was about to refuse Raoul again when someone else answered for him.

"It's me."

CHAPTER 7

ZELDA SWALLOWED AS BOTH GUYS TURNED TOWARD HER. Half of her was demanding to know why the hell she blurted that out. The rest of her was glad to finally have it out in the open. Both parts were terrified of what would happen next.

"You're *what*?" Raoul spat.

She mentally recoiled at his tone but forced her stance to remain steady. "I'm his Mate."

"Him? Really?"

"I was surprised, too." Why wasn't he happy for her? They'd always said that he couldn't wait for the day the other found their Mate. Had he been lying all this time?

"And you didn't tell me? No wonder you've been acting weird whenever I mentioned him. You were already a love-sick puppy!"

"I didn't want things to change between us. And I was worried you'd have a bad reaction like this."

"That shouldn't matter. If you were really brave, you would have come clean immediately. It would have saved our Pack immediately. Instead, you wasted time and us worry for no reason."

"That's enough," Dylan said.

"No," Zelda said. "He deserves to be heard."

Her Mate's expression made it clear he didn't agree with her.

She addressed Raoul. "I know you don't like him as a leader."

"That's beside the point. You're supposed to do what's best for the Pack. And you didn't. The rumors are right. You're just like your brother. Neither of you is fit to be Alpha."

Those last words were the cruelest she'd ever heard.

Before she could blink, Dylan landed a punch to Raoul's jaw, snapping his head to the side. "You don't get to talk to her like that. She is still your *Alpha*."

The man she had trusted her whole life slowly turned his focus back on her Mate and let out a growl before bending forward. She recognized that posture—she'd seen it so many times to mistake it for anything else—he was about to Shift.

Except he didn't. Instead, he let out a howl of pain like she'd never heard before. Not even a first-time Shift was as painful as what she was witnessing. And she wasn't even sure what that was.

"What's happening?" she shouted.

"He can't Shift in here. There's a protective spell on the houses. Get him outside or he'll be ripped apart from the inside."

How was there a spell—? She'd get to that later. Right now, she needed to help Raoul. Zelda ran to Raoul's side before Dylan had even finished explaining. She shouldn't have been surprised when Dylan looped her Beta's other arm over his shoulders before the three of them made their way to the door.

Once outside, Raoul Shifted immediately and attacked Dylan from behind. It was so fast, that Zelda didn't even have time to warn her Mate. She'd never seen Raoul move so quickly or viciously. It scared her more than she ever thought it would.

Dylan, miraculously, was already in wolf form before impact was made. Even if she hadn't known Raoul her whole life, it was easy to distinguish the two men from each other. Raoul was a reddish-brown color while Dylan was gray—almost the same color as her own fur.

When she saw him clamp his jaw down on Raoul's shoulder, she Shifted and did the first thing that came to mind: she attacked her own Mate.

DYLAN IMMEDIATELY REARED BACK IN PAIN, RELEASING RAOUL'S neck. He could feel blood pouring from the wound and already matting his fur. He still remained guarded, though, watching the Equinox Beta's next action.

His attacker was laid out in the grass and Dylan released a low growl when Zelda rushed over to attend to her friend.

He turned tail, Shifted back, and walked into the house. Call him a coward, but he didn't need to watch Zelda fawn over his attacker.

Edon was already waiting for him. He held out a bottle of painkiller, a pack of ice, and supplies for his wound. "I figured you didn't want me to interfere."

"You were right. Anna would come for me if your pretty mug got so much as a scratch on it."

Edon laughed and handed the bottle of antiseptic out.

Dylan grabbed it and poured it over his left shoulder and sucked in a breath. God, that hurt. He touched his collarbone and felt a fracture where it should have been smooth. It was definitely broken, but it felt like a clean break. It definitely could have been worse. And the bite itself stung like crazy. "I wish she had gotten the memo."

"Your *Mate* did that?"

"Did you really think I'd let him get me this bad?" Next, he grabbed the adhesive gauze pad and laid it over the bite. It could still get infected, but it normally wasn't lethal on its own. It was the blood loss that normally killed you. "I got jumped while I had him pinned."

"Man, that's—"

"I don't want to hear it right now, Edon." He tried to use the bandage wrap himself, but the contortion required was too painful. "This thing is starting to hurt."

"Take the meds already, dumbass." His best friend stepped forward and took over the final step of securing the dressing with enough tan bandage layers that Dylan started to look like a Halloween mummy. "No one's going to think you're weak because you did."

His friend handed him the pills and a glass of water. He took them without argument.

"I think we should call our fathers back here. You need to take it easy for a few days so that can heal."

"No. Your dad, maybe. But not mine. Let's see how it plays out."

"Really? How's that working out for you so far? What are you going to do with only one arm in commission?"

"I didn't break my arm. I can still use it."

"That's why you couldn't completely bandage yourself."

He had a point. "I'm serious, Edon."

"So am I. Look, I know she's your Mate, but I don't want you getting hurt. You've already—" He cut himself off when the door opened.

Dylan slowly turned to see a blood-soaked Zelda. She was covered in Raoul's scent and he didn't like it at all. He didn't want to picture how close she'd gotten to the guy to end up so dirty.

It also hit him that she'd been wearing the same few outfits since she arrived. He made a mental note to have Esme and Annabelle take her into town for shopping. Which was a ridiculous thought to currently be having given the circumstances.

"Go shower," he said. "You can use mine. It's upstairs, first door on the right. You can borrow sweatpants and one of my shirts." He fully expected her to refuse but was surprised when she instead changed the subject.

"I'm sorry about that," she said, gesturing to his wound.

He almost said, "I understand," but changed his mind. How she had turned on her own Mate—disregarding the fact that it was *himself*—concerned him. A Mate hurting another wasn't unheard of. Normally it was caused by insanity caused by the werewolf-equivalent to rabies. Was that related to the reason he'd never gone looking for her? Was something wrong with their connection?

And hadn't Fawn also gone through something similar when her angel had been lying? Sure, she wasn't one of them, but soulmates were essentially the same as wolf Mates.

She was still staring at him with an unreadable expression. He hoped he saw some remorse there, and even more so that he'd get an explanation from her later. But knowing her, that wouldn't be forthcoming, and he didn't have the energy to talk in circles until she told him. Without a word, she walked up the stairs. He heard her disappear into his room and let out a breath he didn't remember inhaling.

"All this drama makes me so glad I have Annabelle."

Dylan turned his attention back to his Beta. "I'm sure you are. You're lucky to have her." He smiled. "Otherwise, she's way out of your league."

"You're injured, so you get a pass for such blasphemy. Anyway, she'll probably be stopping by your room tonight with soup or whatever. And who knows what my mom will give you. Please let them dote on you. Or I'll be hearing complaints about it all night."

"Sure thing." Dylan pushed himself to his feet. "I'm leaving you in charge for the rest of the day. If people start talking, tell them the truth except for the part about Zelda and I being Mates."

Edon nodded.

"And as much as I hate to say this, leave Raoul alone to do his thing. I'll set the record straight when I'm better. It shouldn't be on you to do that." With that, he walked upstairs and lay down on his bed, groaning as he landed on his shoulder.

Zelda came out of the bathroom and let out a squeak. "Was this your plan? Entice me into your room and then surprise me?"

He let out a weak laugh that was too painful to sustain more than a second. "No. I need to sleep this off. You're welcome to stay here if you want, but I already know your feelings on the subject."

She shifted on her feet. "I think I'll head back to my Pack."

He just closed his eyes, willing sleep to take him. A moment of silence passed before he heard her walk to the door and leave, closing it behind her.

ZELDA WALKED DOWN THE STAIRS AND SILENTLY OUT the back door, dreading each step she took. When she had left Raoul, he had passed out due to pain and the number of painkillers she made him take, but she still didn't feel comfortable being around him. And sharing a room with him after all that had happened seemed wrong. But spending the night in Dylan's room also didn't sit well with her. She stopped walking halfway between the houses. What was she supposed to do?

Acting on instinct, she turned back around and walked through the first floor until she found Edon talking on the phone in the TV room.

Maybe he knew if there was a neutral territory she could sleep until she figured out her next step. Her hope for that faded when he met her gaze and frowned.

Backtracking, she sat down on the porch of the main house. She didn't see anyone from the Morsure Pack around. It seemed they had all gone into town to work. Maybe Raoul had been right in suggesting their Pack get jobs. They were around, but none of them seemed to notice her. They never did unless she was talking directly to them. It was something that hadn't ever bothered her before but seeing how Dylan's members always acknowledged him, even if it was only by a small nod, made her feel invisible.

Edon stepped out. "Did you want something?"

He hadn't said it rudely, but she could tell it was more forced than his past offers for her to come to him if she ever needed help.

"Is there an empty room here where I can sleep tonight?"

He didn't look surprised by the request. "You'd have to ask Dylan. It's his house. Anything else?"

She shook her head.

"When you get the chance, get some of your Pack to help cook dinner and set the table. Three should be enough. Dylan normally does most of the prep work himself." He rolled his eyes. "But since he's out of commission," his gaze hardened, "we need more people to pick up the slack."

The lump in her throat made it hard to swallow. "Okay."

He didn't say goodbye before he walked back into the house. She heard him climbing the stairs and wondered if he was going to check on his friend and Alpha or was going to tell his Mate everything that had happened.

Zelda's cheeks heated. She probably already heard it all. And her Pack probably did, too. She paled at the thought. If she had just let Dylan tell everyone yesterday, it wouldn't have mattered what they heard because they would know the full circumstances. Then again, they might all start treating her like Edon because she couldn't quite bring herself to regret saving Raoul. He might be suddenly acting out, but he was her friend. Nothing could change their shared past.

She looked back at the house. It was the future that was being a problem. She sighed before walking back to where her Pack was. She found them all in the entryway.

Zelda saw Raoul standing in front of everyone and her stomach dropped. He met her gaze and people started to turn. Some of them gave her sympathetic looks, but most of them glared. One of the guys in her Pack, Hiram, spoke up.

"Is it true?"

"Is what true?"

"That Alpha Stone is your Mate?"

She nodded.

He made a disgusted noise. "Some Alpha you are."

She heard the dissatisfied murmurings and felt her heart speed up. Another said, "Raoul should be our Alpha. Who's with me?"

Zelda froze. He was *encouraging* her Pack to desert her? She took one step back. Then another. She kept going until she was through the doorway and almost fell down the front steps. It was only then that she turned her back and walked as fast as she could back to the main house.

DYLAN HEARD FOOTSTEPS EVEN BEFORE EDON WARNED HIM. He held out his hand, and his friend handed him another painkiller.

Annabelle gave them both scolding looks. "Are you serious? You just had one twenty minutes ago."

"Give me a break. You know we can't go by the human medication recommended dosage. And I have a broken—"

He didn't get to finish his sentence before Zelda barged in. She took one look at him, then at Edon and Annabelle, who gave a small wave. She turned her attention back to him.

Dylan stayed silent. He didn't have anything to say that was nice at the moment and his mother had taught him it was better to be silent than cruel.

"Can I talk to you for a moment?"

"I'm a captive audience."

She winced.

Edon sent him a look over her shoulder. He'd seen it enough times whenever he was fighting with Bailey and his best friend accidentally intruded. It was their shorthand for, *Should I leave?*

He just kept eye contact with him.

Zelda glanced at their audience.

Annabelle started to stand, but Edon placed a hand on her knee, and she settled back down. Her eyes flew to the back of Zelda's head, then to him. He could see she was uncomfortable, but after his Mate had attacked him, especially after he defended her, he didn't feel like being alone in a room with her.

His Mate looked at him again and the guilt in her golden eyes was almost enough for him to spare her the embarrassment of Edon staying in the room. But he didn't.

"Raoul told everyone in my Pack that we're Mates." She paused, and when he didn't respond, she continued. "So, now Dylan and I *have* to do the Ritual."

"Well, don't you sound excited," Edon said sarcastically.

She didn't even roll her eyes at the comment. Her focus stayed fixed on him. As if it was *his* fault.

"You know we can't do it if you don't want to, right?" The consent of both parties was necessary for the Ritual to work.

"Some of my Pack want Raoul to be Alpha instead of me."

His skin heated. It wasn't already enough for the guy to have verbally attacked his Alpha and supposed friend, now he was taking away her birthright, too? "Let them," he bit out. "They'll still be Rogues. I can't help them unless they become part of my Pack, and if they want to give up that protection, it's not your responsibility to stop them."

"As their Alpha, it *is* my responsibility. I didn't put them first earlier, and that's why I'm having this problem."

"You're willing to jump into the Ritual to save them. If they can't recognize you as a good leader, then they're insane and deserve to have that backstabbing ass as their leader."

"I can't believe you would say that about them! They're my Pack."

"Just like he's your friend, right?"

She barged over to his bedside.

This time, Edon didn't ask to leave. Annabelle was right behind him. "You scared our audience away."

"You think this is funny?"

"My Mate attacked me when I went to defend her, and her Beta is a mutinous bastard." He turned his attention from the door and stared at her. "What do you think?"

"Look, I acted on instinct. Raoul and I have had each other's backs our whole lives. You can't blame me for that for the rest of my stay here." She paused. "I need a room to stay in, by the way."

"So, you're still planning on leaving?" When she shrugged, he took a deep breath, swallowing his frustration. "You can take the room next to mine. Will you be waiting out the whole two weeks or leaving in the middle of the night? If you let me know, I can tell Edon to let me sleep through it." He knew it was cruel the moment he said the last part, but seeing her wince made him feel like crap. "That was uncalled for."

"I know I made a mistake. It shouldn't even be possible. But it did. Can't we move on?"

"It depends on you and what you're going to do with your Pack. And Raoul told me that you two have been together. Was that before or after we found out we're Mates?"

"How dare you." She grabbed his pain killers from the bedside table near his good arm and stepped out of reach. "I don't know what he said to you, but we have *never* crossed that line. Not that it would be any of your business if we had."

"I didn't ask. He brought it up. The *real* question is why didn't you? And it is my business because you're my Mate and still sleeping in the same room as him in my backyard."

"Nothing happened. And why do I have to tell you about my past relationships and you don't? It needs to be a two-way street. What about Fawn? *You* never brought her up in conversation."

"We were boyfriend and girlfriend in high school." How many times had he given that simple explanation when he and his father had returned from New York and everyone, especially Edon, wanted to know about his urban life. *How did she even know her name?* It had to be Bailey. Maybe Edon was right and it was time to kick her out. No, he wasn't going to lead his future Pack that way. "And I never kept it from you. You didn't ask."

"Neither did you. Why are you asking now?"

"Because you chose him over me. I'm your *Mate*, Zelda. Nothing is supposed to come between us. And he's still around. Fawn isn't."

"Oh, like that's supposed to make me feel better."

"You know what would make me feel better? Pain meds for my broken collar bone." The last words came out sharply but he was too pissed to feel bad about it.

She had the good grace to flinch. Undeterred, her anger fueled her strong arm as she threw them at him and he caught it with his good hand before she stormed out, the door slamming behind her.

His head fell back on the pillow, sending a sharp jolt of pain through his shoulder. But that was dull in comparison to the ache he felt in his chest from Zelda rejecting their Bond yet again. That could have gone much better.

CHAPTER 8

ZELDA SPRINTED THROUGH THE GRASS SEPARATING THE TWO homes and burst in to see Raoul still holding court as if he were already Alpha. "I need to speak to you."

"Not now."

"As of right now, I'm still your Alpha. Don't make me regret protecting you from Alpha Stone." People gasped, but she ignored them.

He walked into what had been their shared room. "*What?*"

She crossed her arms. "Is that all you have to say to me?"

"What else would there be?"

"How about an explanation for why you're suddenly being such an ass? And don't give me the bullshit excuse of Dylan's arrogance. Because you attacking him was unacceptable. By any standards."

"I'm sick of you always ordering me around." He strode toward her until he was so close to her, she felt him breathing. "You used to treat me like we were equal partners."

"And I want to get back to that. But you're my Beta, and I'm your Alpha. It's my job to do that when necessary. I've only had to because you've been acting out of line."

"Do you really think he'll let you stay Alpha of our Pack? He sure as hell hates me, so I won't be your Beta anymore. Even though I'm the one who's been there for you from the beginning! And yet you've never noticed me."

Zelda stared at him. Had she really missed his interest in her? "You're my best friend. I've trusted you with my life. And, in case you weren't aware, good friends don't suddenly *stop* doing what earned them that title in the first place. If you wanted more, you should have talked to me about it."

"And be shot down? No thanks."

"It would've been better than you building up all this resentment towards me. How am I supposed to trust you now? Regardless of how you feel for me, it doesn't matter because I have a Mate."

She turned and reached for the handle, hesitating when she heard his guttural growl. Then she felt unimaginable pain in her shoulder.

He bit me! was all she could think as he dragged her backward until she was forced to lie on the ground. She could feel her own blood flowing now, staining and making her shirt stick to her. Now she and Dylan had matching wounds. She'd never known karma to act so quickly.

She stared up at her best friend. His face was contorted in a rage she'd never seen before. He looked like a man possessed, and she desperately wished she wasn't frozen in shock. Her dad would be livid. Not just at Raoul, but her for not pegging the threat before the situation got out of hand.

Raoul had been right. Her mind wasn't totally there since meeting Dylan. How had she misjudged both men so badly?

She heard shouting in the main house and running.

Moments later, Raoul was ripped away and out of her field of view.

"I want you gone *now*," Dylan growled. "I'll send one of your Pack members after you with your belongings."

She pushed herself up with her uninjured arm and saw Edon and a broad-shouldered Morsure wolf escort her Beta through the doors. Her arm gave out and she cursed.

Dylan's hand appeared. She grabbed it and pulled herself up.

"Are you okay?"

"Yes. But now I really regret saving him."

He didn't answer, but silently walked her out into the main room and told the wolves who were still there, "I want everyone in your

Pack to know that your Beta just attacked your Alpha, my Mate, because she didn't return his feelings. If he's the type of Alpha you want, you are free to leave my property. You have by sundown to be outside Morsure territory before you are trespassing. But if you stay without being completely devoted to Alpha Makris," he saw Zelda glance at him when he used the title, "you'll wish you'd left with him."

A grumble went through the crowd and some went into their rooms, emerging with what few belongings they had.

"One of you will take your new Alpha's belongings from that room." He pointed. "He left in a hurry and you can meet him outside. Members of my Pack will escort you to the boundary."

Hiram took responsibility. She watched for his reappearance and the others make their slow departure. When they were all outside, away from her, she let the tension in her muscles dissipate.

"It's better this way."

"It doesn't feel like it," she muttered.

"I think you'd be surprised."

Zelda turned and noticed a number of remaining members. She'd been so focused on the ones who left that she hadn't really counted their number in comparison to the rest. God, how bad an Alpha was she really if she was so focused on the wrong thing in this moment of crisis?

She saw Dylan still standing next to her and took a deep breath. To be fair, there were multiple concerns on her plate. With Raoul gone, maybe she'd finally be able to resolve both.

"I just want to first say thank you to all of you. I know I haven't proactively handled the circumstances surrounding our stay here as well as I'm sure you expected me to. In all honesty, I didn't meet my own standards either. For that, I apologize and promise to do better." She glanced at Dylan. "Alpha Stone and I will contact the Council. In the meantime, we will discuss the futures of our Pack. I know none of you signed up for this, but it's what we have to do."

"For the record," one of her she-wolves, Tasha, said, "We never liked Raoul. We're much happier following you."

"I'll let you spend some time with your Pack," Dylan said. "When you're ready, we can contact the Council. Then I'll take you to dinner?"

"I'd like that."

He nodded and left.

"What do you mean you never liked him?" Zelda asked, addressing Tasha and her twin, Tate.

"He might have just now shown his true colors to you, but he's always been coming onto girls in the Pack even when they weren't interested. He never took no for an answer."

He had always told her that the girls were the ones coming after *him*. Was anything they had shared true? "Why didn't you or anyone else tell me? I would have done something about it." It made her stomach clench knowing that he had done that to other members of her Pack—people she was supposed to protect.

"Because you're a good Alpha," Tate said. "But he was our Beta and your best friend. As much as we like you, we couldn't fully trust the outcome." She bowed her head. "No offense."

"None taken."

"And you didn't have to spend most of your speech apologizing," Tasha added. "We all understand it's been tough on you more than anyone. Who could have guessed your brother would die so soon?"

"Well—"

Tasha elbowed her sister in the stomach and Tate shut up.

"You have our full support, Alpha Makris. And not just because the alternative is so much worse."

"Thank you," Zelda said. "That means a lot. Now, if you'll excuse me." She walked to her room and got into the shower, spending extra care to scrub every trace of Raoul away.

She took out her third and last outfit she had—when the Waya Pack had kicked them off their lost land, they hadn't been as generous as Dylan was to her deserters. They had to leave immediately. That she was able to sneak back home and grab anything was something of a miracle.

Fully dressed, she waited outside the big house. A woman opened the kitchen door. "What are you doing waiting out there? Come in."

Zelda had no idea who she was but followed her instructions anyway. "Thank you. And you are?"

"Esme. Edon's mother. So, you're the one who's got our Alpha all tied up in knots."

"I wouldn't say—"

"Why not? There's no denying it's true. Anyone can see it if they know what to look for. Dylan tends to wear his heart on his sleeve."

"He doesn't feel anything deep for me. He can't. We don't know each other that well."

Esme laughed. "You should already know Mates don't work on a normal relationship timeline. And even mortals sometimes experience love at first sight. Knowing each other for a long time is not a pre-requisite, child." She sobered. "But being committed to each other is needed for the Ritual. You know that, right?"

Zelda nodded.

She heard footsteps getting closer and then Dylan's voice. "Esme, leave her alone."

She tensed. How had she not sensed his presence nearby? How much had he overheard?

"Sure, sure. I don't know why you and Edon treat me like I'm a crazy old lady. I mean, I am, but you should still at least pretend you don't know."

If she was crazy, the woman hid it well. Unless she was joking? Esme was inscrutable. Yet another person she couldn't seem to get an accurate read on. Maybe she had spent too long among her own Pack. Her people assessment skills were rusty.

As if reading her mind, Esme turned back to her and winked. "I'm not. It just comes with being their mother. I helped raise our Alpha after his mother died. Anyway, if you ever need anything, come find me. Sometimes a problem needs a woman's touch."

Before Zelda could answer, the woman disappeared back into the house. She saw Dylan staring at her and cleared her throat. "Are we going to contact the Council?"

"We are." He motioned her to follow him into a room connected to the common space. He opened the door for her, then closed it behind them. "The room is soundproof. Not even a werewolf can eavesdrop on anything said in here."

She swallowed. "Great."

"You don't have to look so nervous."

She forced her shoulders to relax. "Been a bit on edge lately."

He didn't comment. He merely pulled out his cellphone. "When you're ready."

D YLAN WAITED FOR ZELDA TO DECIDE FOR HIM to move forward. That seemed to be the running trend in their relationship so far. While he would never push her faster than she wanted to go, he was getting a little tired of constantly convincing her to take the next step. After her speech to her Pack, he thought they were finally on the same page. Which, he now realized, was wishful thinking because his Mate clearly still had reservations. But he couldn't figure out what they were. She hadn't outright said they'd merge Packs, effectively forfeiting her role as Alpha in the process, but her saying they'd contact the Council was declaring the intention all the same. He hit call and put it on speaker.

Elder Kai answered immediately. "Dylan, what can I do for you? I know you are standing in for your father right now, but I didn't expect to hear from you. We've always had complete confidence in your leadership skills."

"Thank you, Elder Kai, but I'm not calling for help. I'm calling to alert you that I've found my Mate."

"That is wonderful news. What's their name?"

"Alpha Zelda Makris, Elder Kai."

There was a pregnant pause. It went on long enough that he wondered if the connection had accidentally dropped. He reached for the phone, but it showed the call was still in progress. Dylan tried to catch Zelda's gaze, but she just stared down at the phone in his hand.

"Congratulations," the man finally said. "The Council is very glad to hear that. We will head to your location and will be there by Friday. I assume your Pack will tell you the details of the Ritual if you have any questions." A voice spoke in the background and Elder Kai added, "I must go now, but you have my congratulations again. We will see you soon." The phone call ended and Dylan stared at the now-dark screen for a few seconds before slipping it back into his pocket.

"Is that all we had to do?" Zelda asked, echoing his own thoughts.

"I'm not sure. But we only have two days to prepare. After we go to dinner, I'll let Edon know and I would recommend you speak to the Mated members of your Pack, too. My father never went too much into the details leading up to the Ritual." It was always painful for his dad to talk about things related to his mom. Dylan tried to spare him as much as possible.

He opened the office door and motioned for her to go first.

Zelda finally looked up from the table at him. "Where are we going?" She asked, walking past him.

"My mom's favorite restaurant. They're vegetarian friendly."

"That's not necessary." Without him having to tell her, she walked out of the house and toward his car.

He unlocked the passenger door just in time for her to pull it open.

Dylan lowered himself into the driver's seat and closed the door. "Well, I've only ordered for you once, and I played it safe by staying away from meat. Just add it to the long list of things I don't know about you. Why don't you shorten it for me?" He opened the door and they walked to his truck. "You've told me about your family, Raoul, and I know you're named after Fitzgerald instead of the video game. I still barely know anything about you. If we're going to do the Ritual—"

" *When*, Dylan. You were just on the call with me." She shut her door with a thud. "There's no *if* about it anymore."

He buckled in, turned the key, and reversed out of the drive. "I want to know more about you. We're going to be binding our souls together. I think we should both go in with our eyes wide open."

"Saying you want to get to know me is great, but it's not specific. And we only have two days, probably less, before we're going to have to be in front of both our Packs and—" She cut herself off and he wondered what she was going to say.

After he parked and they were finally seated with menus and water, he asked, "Why don't you want me to know anything about you?"

"There's really nothing to tell. I'm not hiding anything or making that up. I lived in my brother's shadow, my father taught me how to fight, Raoul was my best friend... My whole life was shaped around them, and now they're all gone. And I'm not ready to step back into a similar situation."

"You think I'm going to make your life about me?"

A few moments passed while she stared at the menu. When she finally lowered the barrier between them, she glanced around to make sure their waiter wasn't close by. "My Pack will be merging with yours and I'll lose my title. How can you view it as anything else?"

"That's cynical." She sounded like Fawn after she first broke up with Caleb. He immediately put the thought out of his mind. Thinking about them right now wasn't a good idea. He needed to stay focused on his Mate.

A waiter approached them. "Ready to order?"

He let Zelda go first, then gave his own.

She took a sip of water before asking, "Will your father be coming back to see the Ritual?"

"I haven't told him yet, but I will when we get back."

"Why haven't you told him yet? If anyone in my family was still alive, I would have contacted them immediately."

Of course, she would have. The circumstances would've been entirely different. She'd have no reason to oppose their Bond.

"You're hiding me." The words were pointed and didn't leave room for him to disagree.

"*I've* been wanting to tell our Packs from the beginning."

"But you haven't told your dad, which means there's a part of you that doesn't want to go through with this."

"No." At least, he didn't think so.

Zelda stared at him and he heard her sharply inhale. "You don't think *I'll* go through with it."

Before he could answer, he felt a painful stab behind his eye and knew that something was wrong with Edon. "We have to go," he said, putting his jacket back on and standing.

"Dylan, we need to talk about this." He never in a million years would have guessed she'd press the topic. Apparently, there was a first for everything.

"We need to get back to the house. Immediately."

This time, she didn't argue, and she stepped out of the booth. He grabbed Zelda's coat and pulled enough money to pay for what they'd both ordered and for wasting the restaurant's time. On his way out, he passed the waiter, whose eyes widened in surprise at their hasty departure. "I'm sorry for the inconvenience. I left cash on the table. Keep the change."

When they pulled up to the house, he threw the truck into park and climbed out. On the porch was a bleeding Edon surrounded by Esme and Annabelle.

Before he could even ask what he already suspected, his best friend muttered, "Raoul ambushed us."

"I'll find him—" Dylan began to turn away, but Esme grabbed his arm, holding his back.

"My son said he took his Pack and left. And before you ask, the others are recovering. There were no fatalities."

"How anyone can follow that asshole is beyond me," Edon said, trying to sit up.

His Beta winced and Dylan felt his friend's pain on top of his own still-healing injury.

Annabelle placed a gentle hand on her Mate's chest and he lay back down without an argument.

What was that like? Dylan wondered.

He sensed Zelda approach from behind. "Are you okay?" she asked Edon.

"I'll be fine," Edon grunted. "Just need to sleep it off."

Esme and Annabelle took the hint and lifted him by placing his arms over their shoulders. Together, they helped him into the house and up the stairs.

Dylan grabbed the bottle of painkillers off the kitchen counter and followed them. He tossed them to Annabelle. "Make sure he takes some, okay?"

"I don't need any," his friend protested. "I'll be fine in the morning. It's already starting to... feel better." He wheezed the last two words.

"It's not negotiable. Besides, you told me to take them." He turned to Annabelle. "Take care of him, alright? Let me know if you need anything else." He kissed her on the cheek then went back downstairs. "And don't let him do anything stupid."

He pulled leftovers out of the fridge and made two plates. One for him and one for Zelda. The night might have gone completely sideways, but that didn't mean either of them had to starve.

When he didn't see her anywhere, he covered hers in wax paper and put it back in the large fridge. "Goodnight," he called to the silent house, then he retreated to his own room and closed the door.

W HEN ZELDA SAW DYLAN KISS ANNABELLE ON THE cheek upstairs, she quickly and quietly retreated to her own room and listened to her Mate in the kitchen. When he said "goodnight" and his own door closed, she went downstairs and found a plate made for her. It warmed her heart. Zelda glanced at the light showing under his door. She was tempted to knock on it, but what could she say to him? They'd ended dinner with her accusing him of not being fully invested in her and their Bond.

He'd practically ignored her once they came back. It was so different than how he'd been on their date, and since they first met. Granted, it made sense for his injured best friend to take precedence and the whole of his attention, but she would be lying to herself if she didn't acknowledge how strange it felt to be almost invisible to her Mate.

She filled a glass of water but had to hold it with both hands, she was shaking so hard. Finding your Mate was supposed to make life easier! But of course, for her, it was the exact opposite. She took a sip. Maybe she was cursed when it came to guys. First her father then her brother were killed, Raoul attacked her, and Dylan... She didn't know what he was yet, but it was definitely driving her crazy.

She heard a door open and spun around, feeling like a teen being caught sneaking back home after curfew. Something she had only done once with Raoul before her dad lectured her so long that she promised not to again just to end the torture.

Esme came downstairs and sat across from her at the kitchen island. "I thought I'd find you down here."

"I'm already that predictable to you?"

The woman made a dismissive sound. "It's a maternal superpower to be extra perceptive."

"Right." She hadn't experienced it in forever, but she remembered how her mother always used to draw out answers from her and Liekos, only to admit she already knew what had happened and merely wanted them to confess.

"Want to tell me what's on your mind? Maybe I can help."

I doubt it. Zelda just smiled and took another sip of her water.

"Didn't peg you for the silent type, or someone who gave up easily, but I've been wrong before. Rarely, of course." Esme winked and leaned in conspiratorially. "But I know I'm not wrong about what I'm about to say, so listen up. Alpha Stone—Dylan—is one of the best men on the planet, and he genuinely cares for you. As I said, anyone would be a fool not to see it. And you would be a bigger fool to throw it away." She straightened and smiled. "But what do I know? My Ritual happened years ago."

"Do you regret it?" The question was out before Zelda could snatch it back. To ask such a thing was one of the worst things you could do, ranking just under disrespecting your Alpha, Beta, or the Pack in any capacity.

"Not for one moment. That's not to say we haven't had some rough patches. Everyone does, but I don't have any regrets about him."

Zelda had never asked her parents if they felt the same way as Esme did. It never before occurred to her to doubt the sacred Bond between Mates. It seemed everyone else had immediately loved each other, and she'd never heard of a couple, including her parents, describe any hesitation on either side at the start of their relationship. Which led her to the sad conclusion that she was the strange exception. She didn't even think Dylan was because his life was normal, and always seemed to be. Hers, on the other hand, was so far from any semblance of normal, it was laughable.

"I'll leave you alone now," Esme said, tearing her out of her mind and back into the present. "But I hope you think about what I've said. Everyone in our Pack wants to see him happy. And you make him happy." She made her way to the stairs. "Goodnight, Zelda."

She watched her go and felt a cold sensation of shame move down her spine. The Morsure Pack had done nothing but be kind to her and her Pack. With Raoul gone, she only needed to focus on the joyous fact of having found her Mate. Her appetite now gone, Zelda cleaned up her unfinished food and trudged to her room and closed the door behind her. Her mind still churning over how to make amends with Dylan, she undressed and climbed into bed. She closed her eyes and reminded herself that nothing else could go wrong tonight.

She thought she heard Dylan say, "Goodnight" from his room across the hall, but she fell asleep before she could overthink it.

CHAPTER 9

DYLAN KNOCKED ON ZELDA'S DOOR FOR THE SECOND time. Breakfast had come and gone, and he hadn't seen her at all this morning. Still no answer. He prepared to knock again, but his hand dropped and landed on the handle as if of its own accord. Turning it slowly, he pushed the door open and glanced inside. He saw her wearing pajamas, lying tangled in the covers, her chest slowly rising and falling. Still fast asleep.

He closed the door and walked back downstairs where he was ambushed by Bailey. "What do you want, Bailey?" He didn't even bother masking his annoyance.

Everyone in the Pack knew how little he liked being surprised. It's not that he couldn't anticipate people, more that he wanted personal space. It was something that Bailey never respected. Yet another reason he was glad they were no longer dating. Although that didn't seem to affect her behavior much given she was practically hanging off him right now.

"Can't I just be a concerned friend?" Her voice was too saccharine to be genuine. Only a fool would assume she had no ulterior motive. But he couldn't guess what she could want from him. "I never got to congratulate you on finding your Mate." She paused and he braced himself for the coming jab. "But I wonder if I'm right to wait to celebrate until after the Ritual. I think everyone might be jumping the gun, don't you think? She strikes me as a runner. She can't handle you or being a leader."

Now he knew where this was headed. "And you can?"

"We both know the answer to that, don't we, Dylan? I know I said some mean things before. And I understand why you broke up with me, but I want you to know there are no hurt feelings on my end."

"I'm glad to hear that. If you'll excuse me."

He tried to move past her, but she laid a hand on his arm, stopping him. "I'm here for you, Dylan. You need me. You know where to find me. I'll always make time for you. As a friend, of course."

Dylan swallowed back the cruel retort sitting on his tongue. One that Esme would no doubt smack him if she even knew he *thought* about saying the words. "That's unnecessary but thank you." Then he more forcefully walked past her.

He found the pair of twins Zelda had spoken to yesterday. "Tasha and Tate?"

They glanced up from their cellphones and looked at him with expectant and wary expressions, respectively.

"Can I talk to you two privately?"

Tasha nodded. Tate silently followed them into his father's study.

"If you're going to talk about our Alpha behind her back—"

Dylan cut Tate off. "This room is soundproof." He took a deep breath and began in a rush. "I know Raoul was Zelda's best friend—"

The twins growled, voicing his own displeasure. He was mildly surprised at Tasha's animalistic reaction. He had the impression she was normally calmer than her twin. Clearly, he wasn't the only one who disliked Raoul.

"But I don't know if she has many other friends in your Pack. I know she might be feeling alone in the current circumstances, and I noticed you both talking to her yesterday."

"What of it?" Tate said.

"I was hoping I could rely on you to be there for her."

"Why wouldn't we be?"

Dylan was speechless. It seemed nothing he ever said was going to make this she-wolf like him. He just hoped she wasn't indicative of the rest of Zelda's Pack. To be fair to her, though, he hadn't spent much time with them since they were all thrown together. He'd barely seen his own members. After the Ritual, he'd make sure to give them more of his attention.

"Of course, we will," Tasha cut in, her tone kinder than her sister's. "We're happy to answer any questions she has for us, but she's a very private person. To be honest, none of us ever know what's she's thinking. It would be a little strange if we went up to her offering advice. She has to come to us first. Our Pack has always operated that way since Alpha Makris' father died."

Tate snorted. "Liekos didn't want anyone contradicting him. He didn't even listen to his own sister." She narrowed his eyes at Dylan. "But why should we help you? I heard you talking to that bitch Bailey. You didn't exactly turn her down when she offered to 'be there for you.' If you're thinking of cheating on Alpha Makris, we won't do a thing to help you. We don't care if that marks us as Rogues. We're loyal to her, not to you."

"What my sister means to say is that we're happy to help our Alpha, but we're going to do what's best for her whether or not that aligns with your goals. I'm sure you can understand our loyalty. After all, the Pack's needs always come first."

"Of course. And thank you."

He let them precede him on the way out and came face to face with Zelda, her hands on her hips.

"Good morning," he said. "You slept late."

She inclined her head toward the twins. "What was that about?"

"We were just talking," he said, and she just stared at him. "I was asking them if it was a good idea to wake you up or to send them. For what it's worth, they nixed both ideas."

"I never sleep in."

He shrugged. "You needed to regroup from yesterday."

She shook her head. "What's the plan for today? The Council is coming the day after tomorrow."

As if he needed the reminder. "I need to speak to Esme about what needs to be done." He wasn't above admitting he needed help.

"You don't already know?"

"Contrary to what Raoul kept telling you, I don't let my pride stand in the way of what needs to be done. I have no problem asking for advice from people who have more experience than me. That's what good leaders do."

"I'm not doing this with you right now. Just tell me when I have to be ready for them. Tonight or tomorrow morning?"

He bit back his frustration. "I think tonight is probably better. There's a full moon tomorrow, so we need to be ready with everything else before then because I believe I remember the final step requiring that. I'm going to ask Esme for more info. You're welcome to ask her any questions you have, too."

A strange look crossed her face, and he wondered if Esme had spoken to her again. "I'll see you tomorrow once the Council arrives."

"Are you going to avoid me until then?" he whispered even though there was a rule in his Pack that forbade wolves from eavesdropping on conversations between Mates.

"I'll see you tomorrow," she repeated.

ZELDA COULD FEEL DYLAN'S GAZE ON HER BACK as she walked back to the guest house. She'd needed a night away from where Raoul attacked her, but it was a new night. Now that he was gone, she'd go back to sleeping in the room she'd originally been assigned. At least until they completed the Ritual. Always being under the same roof as her Mate was beginning to fry her nerves.

He thought she'd been asleep when he'd opened her door that morning, but she had only pretended. She had fallen back asleep between then and coming down for a very late breakfast, but that was beside the point. He had come to check in on her. But it seemed that whenever they were actually talking to each other, they always seemed to be fighting about something.

She was surprised to find the women of her Pack waiting for her in the main area. "Hey," she said, unable to think of anything else.

"We thought we could help with the preparations for the Ritual tomorrow," Tasha said.

"How—?"

"You didn't get the chance to tell us yourself, but that Beta of theirs has a big mouth," Tate said.

"I'm sorry. You should have heard it from me."

Their older sister, Tanya, waved it away. "We knew it would be happening soon. But we have a lot to do."

"I don't really know—"

Maya cut her off. "That's why we're helping."

Tasha spoke up, "If you're okay with that. It was the older generations' idea."

"I'm only ten years older than you."

Zelda smothered a laugh. "No one is calling you old, Tanya." If Tasha was the calm one and Tate was the sour one, Tanya was the sassy one. They'd been her closest female friends in the Pack and she felt guilty for not spending more time with them as they were growing up. "And I'd love all your help," she said. Dylan's words played in her mind, but she quickly shut it down. "What comes first?"

"Lots of cleaning," Tasha answered. "Tonight, we have to take you to a river to cleanse yourself in the light of the original Luna."

"You've got to be kidding me. I don't even—"

"Don't say it," Linda, another, older she-wolf said, "or you can damn your Ritual before it begins. It's been hard enough for both of you so far."

"Someone also needs to buy you a new wardrobe," Tanya said. "I can go with you."

"Trying to get out of housework?" she teased.

"Guilty. So, what do you say?"

"Sure." She paused. "I was thinking of also inviting Annabelle, the Beta's Mate. It's probably a good idea for me to get to know her better. And the sooner we can start familiarizing ourselves with his Pack members, the better."

"If it's going to be a party, I want to come," Tasha said. "Come on, Tate. It'll be fun."

"No thanks," her twin responded.

"Oh, come on. You'll be supporting our Alpha."

Tate's attention swung from her sisters to Zelda. "I better be fed on this trip."

"We should get going. You can't wear those clothes for the cleansing or in front of the Council," Tanya declared.

"Let me get Annabelle first. And I need to ask Dylan if we can borrow his truck."

"I've seen it. There are only four seats in it."

"We can sit in the bed," Tate said. She snickered at her older sister's dismayed expression.

Zelda chuckled, too. "I'll be right back. Grab what you need."

She entered the main house and walked upstairs to Edon's room. She knocked twice. "Who is it?" the Beta responded.

"Zelda."

A moment passed before the door opened. He stood in the doorway. Annabelle was lying on the bed next to the empty side he had presumably just left. She frowned and Zelda hesitated.

"Edon, I'm sick of saying this. Lie back down."

"It's past noon. Dylan needs me to help clean. Too bad he didn't call Alec down. He could do it in five seconds and we'd have the whole day off."

Zelda made a mental note to ask Dylan about who that was in the future. She cleared her throat and Edon turned back to her, seeming to remember her presence.

"Sorry about that. What do you want?"

"I'm actually here for your Mate."

Annabelle stood and walked over, edging herself in front of Edon, forcing him back into the room.

"Babe—" he protested.

The Beta's Mate closed the door behind her, leaving him inside.

Zelda stared for a moment. She hadn't expected to see such a forceful side to Annabelle. Her impression was she was soft-spoken. Definitely in comparison to Esme and Bailey. Although, it made sense when she thought about it. Anyone Mated to Edon needed to have a backbone to balance him out. "Won't he be mad?"

"He'll get over it. What can I do for you?"

"The she-wolves of my Pack want to take me clothes shopping. I was wondering if you or any of the she-wolves in your Pack wanted to join us if you can spare the time. Also, what type of car does Edon have?" She was chickening out on speaking to Dylan and hoped she wouldn't have to ask.

"He has a sedan. Dylan has a truck, though. We can take that. Let me ask the others and I'll meet you in front of the garage. It's next to the gym. You can't miss it. And of course, I have the time. I need to get to know my new Luna, right?"

"Thank you."

She walked downstairs and found Dylan at the kitchen counter reading through a leather-bound book. He looked up and their gazes clashed. She wondered if she'd ever get used to the intensity she always saw in his green eyes.

"Have fun shopping," he said.

Zelda nodded. She saw his shoulders tighten at her nonverbal response. He looked back down and flipped the page.

Clearly dismissed, she walked outside and found the garage. Her Pack members joined her. A few minutes later, Annabelle and three others appeared. They introduced themselves.

"How do you feel about dresses?" one of them asked.

"I—"

"She also needs pants."

Was anyone ever going to let her share her opinion?

"And casual clothes," Tasha said. "Because I might claw my eyes out if I have to keep seeing you in the same three outfits every day." She added the second part in a rush after Zelda turned to her. "Where's a good place to go?"

"There's a mall," Annabelle said. "I can be navigator if the passenger seat hasn't already been called."

"Sounds good to me." Zelda was grateful for her not delving deeper into the arrangement. She looked at the group. "Just don't go crazy on me. I need essentials, nothing else."

Annabelle glanced away.

The hair on her neck stood up. "What?"

"Our Alpha gave us his credit card."

He wasn't her Alpha yet. She held out her hand. "Give it to me."

Annabelle fished it out of her pocket and placed it in her palm.

"Everyone get in the truck. I'll be right back."

She heard Tate let out a whistle as she marched across the grounds. She stormed into the house.

"What are you trying to do?"

Dylan didn't even look up from his reading. "I'm assuming Annabelle caved and told you about it too early."

She grabbed the book from him. "Did you tell her to not tell me?"

He shook his head and held out his hand. "Give it back."

Zelda glanced at the pages and turned the cover. It had no title on it. With his view temporarily obscured, she slipped the credit card into it and slid the book back toward him.

He immediately took it out and pushed it back toward her.

"I don't want to owe you anything."

"You won't. We're going to be part of the same Pack. The resources are open to everyone."

"Don't patronize me."

He didn't bother to deny it again, merely holding the card out until she finally took it.

She shoved it in her back pocket and walked out.

Annabelle was waiting outside Dylan's truck. Everyone else was inside. "Well?"

"Just drive."

D YLAN WATCHED THE TRUCK PULL AWAY FROM THE house and fought the urge to take a nap. He'd come down to the kitchen early that morning before anyone else woke up.

He pulled his phone out and hit speed dial. "Hey, Dad."

"Is something wrong?"

Why did everyone assume that? It might be his first time leading the Pack on his own, but that didn't mean he couldn't handle it. His injuries were already starting to hurt less. "I found my Mate two days ago and the Council is coming tomorrow. Where are you?"

"Nevada, but Connor and I can make it home by tonight. How did you meet her?"

What were they doing there? "Her Pack needed help because they lost territory when her brother was Alpha."

His father didn't miss a beat and picked up on his use of past tense. "She's an Alpha?"

"Yep."

His father hummed in approval. "I can't wait to meet her."

"Before you go... do you have any advice? She's not exactly happy about the situation."

Dylan listened to the dead air. His dad was probably staring at his phone. "What do you mean?"

"We're not seeing eye to eye on a lot of things." That didn't even begin to scratch the surface of what he was experiencing with his stubborn Mate.

"Your mother and I were like that at first."

Wait, what? He'd never heard them say anything negative about their relationship before. "But you were both in love before your Ritual." Dylan regretted saying the words the moment he had.

"And you're not?"

"I don't know. I think I am, but she's constantly driving me crazy."

"That's not evidence that you're not. Then again, I know Bailey drives you crazy. I'm assuming she knows about your Mate?"

"Yes. I broke up with her right before my Mate arrived."

He could practically hear his father nodding. "I'll see you soon. Congratulations, son. I'm sure she'll come around."

The call ended. Dylan shoved his phone back in his pocket and dropped his head into his hands.

"Tough morning?"

Under the table, he kicked the stool out so Edon could sit. "You could say that. What about you?"

"I'm fully healed, same as you. Though, why you weren't bed-bound for as long as I was is a mystery."

"I didn't have a Mate hovering over me the whole time. And I think your mom gave up on keeping me in one place."

"Which would normally never happen. Did you pull Alpha rank on her or something?"

"Like I'd ever try that. I think she knew that I needed to be on the ground floor working things out."

"How's that going?"

He leveled a glare at Edon.

"That bad, huh? Can I do anything to help?"

"Tell me how to prepare for this."

"You were there with me, dumbass."

"My mind has been a bit preoccupied since then, *dumbass.*"

"Right. That whole trip to New York to help your ex."

"You know I don't feel that way about Fawn anymore."

"Are you sure? Is there any part of you running toward the Ritual so you can finally close that chapter?"

"Don't tell me you're buying into Bailey's gossip."

"Of course not. I'm not an idiot. My observations are my own."

"Then you need an eye doctor. Now, seriously, what do I do?"

"Clean like the Plague is here, let go of any past romantic relationships, fill up on food, and wear white clothes. Don't forget, you have to purify yourself in the lake tonight."

"That's it?"

"Before tomorrow? Yeah. The rest is to suck up to the Council. Especially having a feast."

"I don't have time—"

"My mom's already shopping. Don't worry about it."

"The moon won't reach its apex for hours. So, I'm just supposed to sit here and look pretty?"

"Please. You're way too ugly for that."

"Shut up." Dylan closed the Council's Lawbook, which also contained the more complicated concerns around the Ritual while lacking any specifics in the preparation leading up to the defining moment of werewolves. "You want to help me? Let's go sparring."

"You know you can't punch out every problem, right?"

"Of course, I do. Now shut up and get on the mat."

CHAPTER 10

ZELDA KICKED THE KITCHEN DOOR CLOSED, COUNTING FIVE Morsure Pack wolves cleaning the first floor on her way toward the stairs.

She dropped four full shopping bags onto the guest room floor in what was her current and only refuge in the crazy set of circumstances that were now her life. For the next two weeks, she reminded herself. She doubted Dylan would *let* her stay in a separate room once the Ritual was over. Married humans sometimes did, but it was unheard of for wolves.

Zelda kicked off her shoes and walked to the window. It seemed every wolf from both Packs were cleaning everything. She didn't remember ever doing this much when other members of her Pack had their Rituals. Maybe it was because it was an Alpha Ritual? She shook her head. It shouldn't matter. Aside from the title and greater responsibility, her father had always taught her that all wolves in a Pack should be more or less equal. Wouldn't that naturally extend to their most important tradition?

A knock at the door pulled her back to Earth. "Who is it?"

"Annabelle. You disappeared on us. Can I come in?"

Zelda opened the door and found her new best friend from her Mate's Pack standing there with a plate filled with a lobster po' boy and fries in one hand and a bottle of water in the other.

"I thought you might be hungry again."

"We just ate. And where did you get that?"

Annabelle just held the plate out to her.

Zelda's stomach growled, and she grabbed the food. "You didn't answer my question."

"Dylan made it for lunch. I'm surprised there were any leftovers. If you ask me, he probably set this aside for you."

Zelda took a bite and held in a groan. It was so good.

"Oh, and in case anyone didn't tell you, tonight you have to drink a potion of sorts while bathing in the moon-illuminated pond in the woods. It's a Morsure Pack tradition. You look like you're ready to fall asleep," Annabelle commented, looking her over. "Long day?"

Zelda nodded. "I've never been one for shopping." She took a long sip of water. "It's embarrassing that walking around a mall was so exhausting."

"Nah. I felt the same way when Esme and Cassidy dragged me out to get my Ritual dress. She doesn't even *like* shopping and she went all in."

"Who's Cassidy?" Was that another of Dylan's exes?

"Edon's older sister. Her Mate's Pack is in Colorado. You'll meet her when she visits next."

"Speaking of meeting people... What is Alpha Makris like? Dylan hasn't talked about him a lot. Do they not get along?" *Had he even told his dad about her yet?*

"They're pretty close."

"May I ask why he isn't here with his Pack?"

"He wanted to take some personal time and also to give Dylan a chance to lead. I'm pretty sure he talked Connor, Edon's dad, into doing the same. Edon's been checking in with his dad from time to time, but Dylan hasn't."

"I don't understand. Why not?"

"He wants to prove himself and thinks asking for help is cheating."

Zelda tried not to flinch at that. It seemed she and her Mate had that perceived flaw in common. "Do you know if they're coming?"

"Of course." Annabelle narrowed her eyes. "Unless you know of a reason why they wouldn't be in attendance?"

She'd heard how Edon's Mate gave Dylan hell for not taking pain meds yesterday. And despite the issues she had with her Mate, Zelda wasn't about to unleash the surprisingly potent wrath of Annabelle on him again.

"Just didn't know how far they had to travel. It's happening *tomorrow*, after all."

"They'll be here."

But would they be happy to meet her?

D YLAN TURNED UNDER THE SHOWERHEAD, WINCING AS THE hot water pelted his injured shoulder along with the new bruise forming on his rib cage thanks to a dirty hit Edon had landed during their fight. Though he was fully healed, his shoulder was still very sensitive. The punch hadn't hurt too badly, but the ass had the nerve to justify it by saying, "It's what he would have done."

There wasn't any point in thinking about Raoul anymore, so Dylan had left it at that. If you disregarded him chucking his water bottle full force at his Beta's head. His friend had easily dodged it, so it didn't matter either way.

But he would need more painkillers. Which was what hurt him more than anything. He didn't want to imagine what his dad would say about his injuries. Especially not a rundown on how he could have avoided them altogether.

This wasn't a boxing match his dad was coaching. It was something much more complicated that didn't follow any rules. Even sacred ones.

Dylan looked down to where his fingers were pruning. He'd been hiding away long enough. He braced himself as he turned the shower's temperature from hot to cold. He counted to ten, then shut the whole thing off and stepped out. He rubbed his hair with the towel before wrapping it around his waist and looked out the window at the progress below. The grass had been mowed and four wolves, two from his Pack and two from his Mate's were setting up the giant tent where he and Zelda would be tended to after the Ritual as they healed under the Council's supervision. The sun was starting to set and he had a feeling the Packs would call it quits soon.

He turned away and got dressed as he wondered where he would house the five Council members. As far as he knew, Stella's modifications didn't let anyone alter the layout anymore than what she had already done. He'd have to ask his dad once he arrived.

Dylan heard footsteps outside his door and opened it.

"Is your father on his way back?" Annabelle asked.

"He'll be here by tonight. So will Connor."

"I'm sure Esme will be glad to hear that."

Dylan smiled. "Is that all?"

"Are you taking your pain meds?"

"Anna—"

"Just do it, Dylan. You're going to be bit again tomorrow. You need to be fully healthy or—"

"It won't work. Yes, I know."

"So, you'll do it?"

He sighed. "See you later, Anna."

She turned, then paused. "You just had to give Edon a black eye, didn't you?"

"We were sparring! I'm not allowed to do anything today, so I needed him to distract me. It's not my fault he let his guard down. And it's not as if he didn't land a bunch on me, too."

"Oh, I know." She shook her head. "Men," she muttered, "always injuring yourselves or each other. No wonder girls are smarter. You punch out all your brain cells. Zelda wasn't happy about feeling the hits in the middle of shopping. Speaking of," she added, "you should spend some time with her. Go out to dinner, or something. Don't forget, we'll be fasting all day tomorrow."

Edon had mentioned it when he kicked Dylan out of the kitchen after making lunch for everyone. All the wolves, who were normally quick to devour food, were positively ravenous.

"Go find her, Dylan. I think it'll be good for you."

He wasn't disagreeing. It was Zelda who normally put a stop to those plans. "I'll ask her."

Dylan tugged on a pair of sweatpants and knocked on Zelda's door.

She opened it and paused, her focus dropping to his chest.

His muscles tightened under her heated gaze.

Her eyes continued their perusal, sliding down the length of his body before she raised them again to meet his.

Caught, she froze for a second and retreated into the room.

Dylan debated entering the room, but he didn't want to crowd her. It might be his guest room, but it was her temporary sanctuary. He watched Zelda bend over and rummage in one of the shopping bags, barely holding in his pained groan. Her new pajamas left little to the imagination at this angle. Not that he'd tell her.

She turned back to him and held out his credit card. "This is yours. I hope we didn't put you in too much debt."

Truth be told, he'd been watching the charges come through on his phone and hadn't been worried even when she threatened to bankrupt him. Bailey, in her position, would definitely have cleaned him out.

He slipped it into his pocket. "I was hoping we could try for another dinner date. We don't start fasting until midnight."

"I was hoping for a night in."

He pulled up the food app. He handed it to her. "You pick."

Moments passed as she scrolled through the items. She gave the phone back to him and squeezed past him on her way to the hallway. "You still have vodka left, right?"

He closed the door behind them and followed her, completing the order as they walked to the kitchen. "My dad's coming home tonight. We probably shouldn't be drunk when he arrives."

His Mate opened the fridge and grabbed two cans of ginger ale instead. She held one out to him and he took it. She opened hers and took a big sip.

He couldn't help but focus on her lips when she licked the excess drops off them.

"So, what did you want to do in the meantime?"

"We can watch a movie. Although, that's better in one of the bedrooms. If we watch out here, who knows who'll join in."

She sent him a look, but he refused to look away. She finally did and let out a huff. "Fine. But nothing stupid. And we each stay on one side of the bed."

"Bed, huh? I was going to suggest we sit on the floor with cushions and blankets."

She didn't answer and surprised him when she turned into his room instead of hers.

He gently closed the door and folded his blanket down.

Wordlessly, she climbed into the side closer to the window and he took up his normal spot.

They had just settled in to watch when his door opened, announcing his father's arrival.

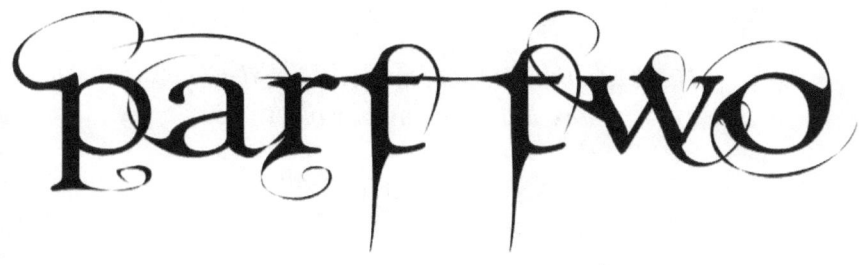

*Those are the voices of my brothers, darling;
I love the company of wolves.*

ANGELA CARTER

CHAPTER 11

ZELDA JUMPED OUT OF BED. THIS WAS *NOT* how she wanted to meet her Mate's father, the true Alpha Stone.

Dylan, on the other hand, was much calmer. He didn't even move when he said, "Hey, Dad."

She held out her hand and approached her future father-in-law. "Nice to meet you, Alpha Stone."

She heard Dylan release a frustrated breath but didn't turn around to check on him. What did he expect her to say? He had told her himself that his father owned the title, especially now that he was back.

He didn't say anything for a moment. Merely staring at her until she shifted on her feet. "A pleasure to finally meet you, Alpha Makris."

His voice sounded strained. Was he that relieved that Dylan had found his Mate? Or was it something else? Because it didn't really seem to her that the Morsure wolves were pressuring Dylan to find his Mate as much as her Pack had been. Then again, his Pack didn't have a past Alpha who seemed unhinged.

"The Council will be arriving tomorrow and your lives will be bound together once the full moon begins to set." He said casually, but the words made her breath stick in her lungs. "Are you ready for that?" He looked directly at her as he voiced the question, and Zelda felt her throat close.

She startled when she felt a hand on her back and she turned to see Dylan standing next to her. She hadn't even heard him move.

"We are," Dylan answered his father.

Marcus didn't look convinced but also didn't voice his reservations out loud. "Then I'll see you both tomorrow."

"You're turning in already? It's not even nine o'clock yet."

"You both should go to sleep early, too." He walked away, and Zelda listened to his footfalls move further down the hall to his room.

Dylan wordlessly dropped his hand from her back and started remaking the bed.

"What are you doing?"

"I figured you'd want to go back to your room now."

"Are you kicking me out?"

He didn't even glance at her. "Nope."

"Then why don't you want me here?"

He tugged the blanket with more force than necessary, creating a new crease. It was the only sign of tension she could find in him. Even his voice sounded even as he said, "You're putting words in my mouth." He walked around the bed, giving her a wide berth as he did so, and fixed his mistake.

He grabbed a leather-bound book, the same one she had seen him looking at when he gave her his credit card that afternoon and leaned against his headboard. Then he began reading again.

Zelda walked around the bed and sat next to him, leaning over to see the pages. She wouldn't make it *that* easy for him to ignore her.

Handwriting filled them and she could immediately tell it was someone's journal. The entry's date was smudged, but she could still read the contents. It was about preparing for the Ritual, and what the writer and his female Mate had to go through. It mentioned the same drink that Annabelle told her about. She read through the ingredients. Individually, she didn't mind them, but all together? It would be like eating Italian and Indian, two cuisines she loved, at the same time. Her stomach soured at the thought. She'd probably throw up before she could get the whole drink down. And they had to drink it while skinny-dipping in a pond? Talk about uncomfortable.

"Who wrote that?"

He turned the page. "My dad."

She lifted her head to look at him. Then at the door where the man in question had gone. She thought about the similarities between the two. They physically resembled each other, and she wondered if father and son also viewed the Ritual and Mates the same way. Dylan acted similar to Marcus' journal, but Marcus hadn't seemed happy she was there. Did her Mate pick up on it or was she being paranoid?

"I don't think he likes me."

"He doesn't know you yet."

"Neither do you." The moment the words were out of her mouth, she regretted them. Of course, he didn't. She wasn't giving him any opportunities.

His phone buzzed and he left without a word.

Zelda watched his retreating back and wondered if something had happened today while she was out. She'd seen Dylan frustrated with her before, but never cold to her. She'd never been worried about him going through with the Ritual before, but now she couldn't help but wonder. He might have told his father everything was moving along smoothly, but what if he was having doubts?

But she hadn't noticed the change until Marcus arrived. Were there problems between the two of them that Dylan hadn't told her about? She tried to remember if Dylan appeared scared of his father but couldn't clearly visualize his expressions from the short conversation. *What if Marcus hurt Dylan? What if—?* Before she could spiral even further, Dylan came back holding a pizza box. He placed it on the bed between them.

She must have left some of her doubt show because he met her eyes and sat back down slowly. "You okay?"

She cleared her throat. "Fine. I forgot the pizza was still on its way."

"Meeting my dad threw you for a loop, huh?" He sounded more relaxed, but his jaw was tight.

She wanted to reach out and hold him, comfort him somehow. She barely resisted the urge and sat on one hand. "I wasn't expecting it so soon. Which is silly, because I knew he was coming home tonight." She tipped back the can of ginger ale and counted to three before she finished her large sip. She'd have hiccups later, but she could live with that.

"You being surprised doesn't reflect badly on you. I didn't know what time he'd get here, either. My dad probably wanted to be here before the Council." He paused. "Are you ready for tonight?"

Zelda glanced out the window. It was still early enough that she couldn't even see the moon yet. "How big is the pond?" Would they be seeing each other naked tonight? Would the other wolves? She'd never been ashamed of her body, but that didn't mean she was comfortable with the idea of her current and future Pack members seeing her skinny dip. Even if it was for a time-honored tradition.

He stared at her for a moment and she felt the urge to shift. She forced herself to stay still while she waited for him to respond. He dropped his gaze to the pizza box and he grabbed another slice. Before taking a bite, he said, "Big enough for about ten people. Never counted before. You know it'll just be the two of us, right?"

"I wasn't sure. My Pack doesn't have this tradition." When she didn't answer, Dylan added, "We're not *together* tonight. It's all about cleansing ourselves and our past relationships so we're ready to commit to each other at the Ritual." He paused, frowning. "I guess you could call it a baptism."

He didn't sound fond of the term.

"Not religious?" She asked.

"Friend had a bad experience with God and the Devil. I'm now a lot less inclined to believe either of them is that great."

She wondered which friend he was mentioning.

"It's a long story. Anyway, tonight probably won't take more than twenty minutes. Depends on how fast you can take a bath."

Zelda couldn't recall ever doing something so decadent. She would probably be done in five minutes. Once her mom died, she and her dad became very functional. Anything else was considered extraneous.

The only reason she had any dresses before she went shopping was there had been celebrations for other newly united Mates in her Pack. Everyone had been expected to dress up for those feasts, and her father had relented in her getting three dresses. She'd had to sell two of them, but the green one she still had from her home was her favorite. It reminded her of one her mother used to wear.

She was curious about how long Dylan would take. She wouldn't *watch* him, but she wondered if he would watch. He was always caring about her movements. Oh, who was she kidding? She was curious to see him in the moonlight after seeing him in a towel.

"We still have time for a movie or to start watching a series before we have to go outside," Dylan said. He glanced at the can in her hand. "I'll get you more, first." He plucked it from her hand and walked out of the room, adding over his shoulder, "You can browse on the TV. I'm already logged into my streaming accounts."

DYLAN ENTERED THE KITCHEN. WHEN HE'D HEARD HIS father's voice asking him to talk, he knew something was wrong. At first, he'd ignored his dad's request. Something he had never done before but he hadn't wanted to sacrifice any time with Zelda. They'd had so little time together and the Ritual hinged on them being open with each other. Tonight, was their last real chance to do so before they also had to cleanse themselves of their pasts.

It was a losing battle from the start because he had barely been able to pay attention to his Mate over his father's voice in his head. But his father wouldn't be denied and had kept mentally hounding him, with increasing insistence, until he finally gave in.

He'd told Zelda he was grabbing them drinks. And he would, but that had to come second to whatever his dad wanted. And not because Marcus was Alpha, but because his father never asked him for trivial things. He debated grabbing a beer for himself but opted for filling his water bottle. He'd been so tense lately that staying hydrated apart from his workouts has turned his stomach.

He closed the fridge.

"Are you trying to scare me, Dad?" He'd heard his father enter, but his dad hadn't said anything. Dylan had learned to be straightforward from his father, but right now Marcus was uncharacteristically silent. "What did you want to talk about?"

He expected his father to speak, but again he heard his dad's voice in his mind rather than through his ears. *I don't think you should go through with the Ritual.*

"What? You can't just say that, Dad. You have to tell me why! Why would I *ever*—?"

His father pointed to his ear, and Dylan cut himself off.

He briefly wondered if God had somehow moved his meddlesome attention from Fawn to him. What else could explain everything going wrong so quickly? And why would God take any issue with him? He and his Pack and had helped clean up the demon invasion mess in Manhattan. You'd think God would have thanked him by making his life easier, not harder. His Mate had been impossible to find and once they finally met, she attacked him. Now his dad was telling him to do the exact opposite of what he wanted and what was expected. Which was insane because his father was the foremost champion of rules he'd ever known. Especially those set by the Council.

Dylan closed his eyes, grounding himself. He was standing in the kitchen with his father, and his Mate was upstairs, completely un-aware that his dad was trying to talk him out of completing their Bond.

Why not?

His father looked away. *I know we've all wanted you to find your Mate, but I had no idea it would be her.*

What does that even mean? Do you know her family? She said her dad knew you.

We were friends.

It was like pulling teeth, trying to get answers from him. What had happened to his father who never skirted an important question?

Even if I agreed to do you what you're asking—which I'm not—*it's too late. The Council will be here tomorrow.*

They would understand.

Okay. He started hating the Devil once he learned about him mess-ing with Fawn, and once he'd been defeated, he'd done his best to ex-punge religious epithets from his language. But, really, what in blazing Hell was going on? What could possibly be so serious that not only his father was willing to disobey Council law but also the Council *themselves* would allow it to happen?

Before he could ask again, his father told him, *Believe me, son. I want what's best for you. If you go through with the Ritual tomorrow,*

I can't protect you from what will follow. He turned and started climbing the stairs.

Whatever his dad was thinking, it couldn't be any worse than what Fawn had gone through. Her soulmate had literally sent her to Hell. And Dylan already experienced what it was like to have his other half betray him.

He grabbed a can of ginger ale from the fridge and his water bottle before running up after his dad.

Marcus was about to enter his bedroom when Dylan cleared the last step.

I'm going through with it, Dad. I hope to see you there tomorrow with everyone.

His dad didn't turn around or answer. He disappeared into his room like a ghost and Dylan wondered if the whole situation had to do with his mom. It was the only time his dad was secretive. But what did his Ritual have to do with his parents? Theirs had gone fine—they'd been happy and eventually had him—so why did Marcus think his would go horribly wrong?

CHAPTER 12

ZELDA HAD GIVEN UP ON HEARING HER MATE'S conversation with his father almost immediately.

She heard the doorknob turn and quickly glanced out the window as if she'd been staring out it for a while.

When the door closed, she turned to her Mate and immediately noticed the dark circles under his eyes and the slowness of his stride.

He held out her ginger ale. "Sorry it took so long."

Honestly, she'd completely forgotten about it. "Thanks." She took a small sip, watching him do the same from his metal bottle. Even though she desperately wanted to know whatever was going on between him and Marcus, it was their business. She hadn't always gotten along with her own father, but she'd give anything to have him with her now. She wondered what he would've thought of Dylan.

"Are you okay?"

She focused on her Mate, who was staring at her with concern shining in his eyes.

She blinked back her tears. "I was just thinking about my family."

"Are you sad they won't be here tomorrow?"

"I actually really hadn't thought about that until now. It's not that I don't miss them, but..."

He nodded. "I get it. A few years ago, I stopped wishing my mom could be alive now. It just hurt too much to always wonder what life would be like with her around now. Or what my life would have been if she'd never died."

"Well, I guess you're stronger than me, then. I still sometimes dream about that."

"It doesn't mean that at all. We just handle our grief differently."

He was right. They were different. But the more time she spent learning about his family, the more she saw some strange similarities between them.

They sat there, staring into each other's eyes for a few more moments. She looked away first, unable to stand up to the intensity of his gaze. Even without the Ritual, she felt like Dylan already had a way to see into her soul.

She pointed to the TV. "I picked a movie," she said, changing the subject. "I've never seen it before, though."

Dylan turned his head and let out a surprised laugh. "You're kidding me. How have you never seen it? You're telling me no one ever had you watch this series?"

She shrugged. "I guess you'll make sure I do." It was the first time she talked about their future together in concrete terms. Did he notice?

He shrugged. "Let's get through the first one. If you don't like it, then we don't have to go through the other seven."

D YLAN GLANCED OVER AT HIS SLEEPING MATE AND sighed. The credits were rolling and she'd completely missed the second half. It wasn't a sign she hated it, but it wasn't an encouraging one either. Maybe he'd try again after their lives had settled down.

Come in, he mentally said.

Edon stuck his head in and took in the scene. *It's almost time. Should Anna bring up the smoothies?*

Dylan grimaced. He wasn't looking forward to this part. And his friend calling it anything but a potion just emphasized how unpleasant this would probably be. Edon was a positive person, but he had tells for when he was overdoing it on purpose. This was one of those times.

Let's just get this over with. You and Anna should be here in case you have to force me and Zelda to finish it.

He didn't want to wake her. It would bring an end to her leaning against him, her head resting on his shoulder. "Zelda," he murmured.

She didn't stir.

Zelda, he tried again.

She sat up immediately, her eyes wide with panic. She glanced him, then Edon in the doorway.

"Anna's on her way with the special drinks," Edon said. "Then it's time for you both to head down to the lake for some skinny dipping."

Did he imagine it or did Zelda's breath hitch at that?

The door opened and his stomach knotted.

"It helps if you breathe through your nose while you do this," Anna said.

He held his hand out and immediately began drinking it before even Zelda had hers. He counted the seconds of his inhale, then his exhale, and repeated. Only when there was no liquid left did he put down the glass. His stomach tried to revolt, but he swallowed it down.

Edon let out a low whistle. "Damn. That was hardcore."

"You would say that." Annabelle turned to Zelda, who looked as green as the potion they had downed. "He had to keep pausing."

Edon grabbed the glasses, his nose wrinkled and fear in his eyes, probably remembering his own experience. "Well, have fun you two."

Annabelle grabbed Edon's arm and pulled him through the door.

Dylan glanced out the window. If they didn't get out of the house soon, there'd be an issue. The full moon was the only time wolves couldn't control the Shift. And he didn't want Zelda to go through the pain of being trapped in the process. "We should go soon."

He saw understanding dawn on her features.

Don't do it, Dylan, he heard his father.

He ignored the voice. This was his Mate. It was his destiny. And he'd learned from watching Fawn what happened when you tried to fight it.

ZELDA STOOD AT THE EDGE OF THE LAKE and shivered. Not because the temperature was cold, or even that there was a breeze. No, it was because she could feel Dylan's gaze from all the way across the water. She could see him clearly and had no doubt he could, too.

She dropped the towel and quickly waded in until she was neck-deep. Then she swam to the moonlit section of the lake. The trees blocked the moon enough that it was a rather small area in the center of the pond. Had it been much smaller, she and Dylan would be so close, they'd probably be touching.

He'd explained the tradition on the way over while they were running in wolf form. They had to be in the lake until the moon left the apex. She had no idea how long that would be and just hoped her limbs wouldn't get tired from treading water before it was over. The most important part of the whole thing was letting the moon purify them of past relationship baggage. Anything that could affect theirs before it started. His tone hadn't changed, but she knew he was thinking of Raoul when he'd shared that part.

Zelda wondered if he had much work to do about Bailey, but she dismissed it. He seemed closer to Viv than to the she-wolf. But Bailey had also mentioned Fawn, her Mate's first girlfriend. Then again, Edon had told her to basically ignore everything Bailey said. Though she wasn't sure if that was out of solidarity with Dylan or if it was really because she was lying, and he didn't want her to listen to gossip.

But she needed to focus on her own. Not his.

Dylan swam up and she went under, unable to meet his likely curious and probing gaze.

She thought of Raoul. Their friendship, his unrequited love, and the utter betrayal. She exhaled, imagining all the bubbles taking away the hurt he caused. Once her lungs were burning, she resurfaced.

She turned her head toward the sky. The moon was still high, a bright spot in the otherwise dark space. She'd been in a city for so long, she couldn't remember even the most obvious signs of celestial entities changing position.

Zelda felt his gaze on her and lowered her gaze from the sky. When their eyes met, she felt a shiver run through her and a sudden pull at her chest, urging her to move closer. Before she could think twice about it, she did exactly that. Before she completely closed the distance, she stopped herself, gritted her teeth, and continued to tread water. Being any closer to her Mate would probably drive her mad and make her do something she wasn't ready for yet. They were already practically touching, it wouldn't take much for her to give in to the sudden need to kiss him. And she had a feeling it wouldn't stop there based on the heat she could see in his eyes.

He moved fractionally closer. It was such a small change, that it shouldn't have affected her more than she already was, but it did.

Zelda forced herself to take a deep, calming breath, but his scent overwhelmed her senses. His nostrils flared, and she wondered if he was experiencing the same thing.

They stared at each other for a moment that seemed to go on forever. For the first time, she didn't immediately look away, and she was able to really see the depth of his green eyes. They were mostly forest green while the moonlight reflecting off the water lit up parts of his irises to the point they appeared to be a bright emerald.

It wasn't until her hand accidentally touched his arm, that she realized they'd moved even closer without her knowing.

He looked away first. But rather than backing away or dropping his gaze down, his gaze seemed to jerk and settle on something behind her.

Her hair stood up and she glanced behind herself. She scanned the edge of the lake and the tree line but couldn't see anyone. She still felt like she was being watched. She turned back to him and waited for him to say something, but moments passed in silence. Then he turned and swam back to his side.

She took the cue to do the same and grabbed her towel off the branch she'd left it on. That had been surprisingly intense and she was glad it was over.

D YLAN HADN'T RUN INTO ZELDA SINCE THEY RETURNED to the house. He'd seen her panicked look when he'd moved closer. He'd tried to fight the urge, but it had taken too much strength to do that *and* keep his head above water, so he'd given in.

She clearly needed space and he wasn't going to be the ass who crowded her. He just wished she'd be more open with him. Every time he felt like they made a connection, she ran, and he wondered if it had even happened or if it had all been a fever dream.

Dylan knocked on his father's door.

"Come in."

"Something weird happened just now."

His father's gaze sharpened. "Tell me."

"Zelda and I were in the lake and I felt like we were being watched. But there weren't any wolves around. Or humans. Or even witches. And we both know the only angel on Earth is in New York or London, or wherever with Fawn."

Marcus didn't seem surprised. "You just had a feeling. Nothing actually happened?"

"No."

"Stay vigilant. This is just the start of what I was talking about."

"I still have no idea what that is because you won't tell me. We never used to keep things from each other. You went on a vacation without much notice and now you're asking me not to go through with the Ritual. If you know something important, why can't you tell me?"

"Because I can't, Dylan. I wish I could. But I swear I can't. And there's nothing to be done about it now. It happened a long time ago. That's all I can say."

Dylan sighed. "I wish I could believe you, Dad."

When Marcus didn't come up with a rebuttal, he turned and went back to his room. He pulled the journal out from under his pillow and flipped forward to the Ritual. And then immediately regretted it. No child should ever have to read about their parents' first time together. He quickly flipped through the rest of the book until it was safe to read again. It described the utter bliss they felt in each other's presence.

He glanced at his closed door, imagining Zelda in her room. Would he ever have that with her? Or were they going to be the one werewolf couple which complete happiness eluded?

CHAPTER 13

Zelda brought the fresh cup of coffee to her lips. "Thank you, Alpha Stone."

He didn't acknowledge her and simply sat back down at the head of the table, Dylan to his right. Edon and his family also sat with them.

"The Council should be here any minute." He didn't sound happy, but no one in Edon's family commented on it. She still couldn't figure out why Marcus wouldn't be as happy as the rest of the Pack was about Dylan finding his Mate.

Did the others at the table know why? Or were they just keeping their noses out of it? But Dylan being eligible to become Alpha affected the whole Pack, especially them. There were rare cases where Betas became Alphas in the event that there wasn't another Alpha to take over for the last one. If Edon became Alpha because Dylan had to step down, would her Pack still be allowed to merge with the his?

She'd be lying if she said it was the only reason but saving her Pack was a large reason she was going through with this so quickly. And Dylan knew it.

If they'd met under different circumstances, maybe they'd have more time to date and actually fall in love before they had to complete the Ritual, but that clearly wasn't what life had in store for them. She just hoped she was doing enough as Alpha, and that her Pack forgave her for keeping the whole thing a secret in the first place.

"Zelda."

She blinked, focusing on Dylan. From the sound of it, he'd been calling her name for a bit.

"Sorry, what?"

"The Council is on its way. The Ritual will happen at sundown," Marcus explained, giving her an indecipherable look. It wasn't anger or disappointment, but whatever it was, it wasn't positive. "The feast will immediately follow. Thank you, Anna and Esme, for working so hard on the food."

"We helped," Edon muttered.

Alpha Stone directed his attention to Dylan and her. "Make sure to be on time. If all goes well, the Ritual will take no more than fifteen minutes."

Out of the corner of her eye, she saw her Mate sit straighter, his muscles tensing as if preparing for a fight. She also caught Connor and Esme exchanging an uneasy glance. So, *they* knew what was going on, but she didn't.

She hated going into situations blind. And that seemed to be the only thing she'd been doing since coming to New Orleans. She couldn't wait until she was back in control of her own life, but she had a sinking feeling it wouldn't be for a long time. If it ever came at all.

D YLAN STARED OUT THE WINDOW AND WAITED FOR the Council to arrive. *What was taking them so long?*

"You know that won't make them arrive faster, right? Think they'll want you to break up like your dad?"

Dylan shot him what he hoped was a withering look, but his Beta kept talking.

"I mean, the Council *has* to know about what happened. And I doubt they want two werewolf lines to be ended at once."

"The curse doesn't say death happens before a new generation is born. I think that's kind of the point. Perpetual punishment as the ultimate screw you."

Edon nodded. "Hadn't thought of that. But you still didn't answer my question. Do you think they'll refuse to preside over a Ritual?"

Was that even possible? He'd never heard of it happening before, but then again, he'd never thought it was possible for a Mate to turn on one another and that had happened. And maybe the witches' curse had made rendered werewolf precedent useless.

"I don't know," he muttered. He took a deep breath, forcing his heart rate to slow down. "Is Annabelle with Zelda?"

"I know she was earlier. But if she's supposed to babysit your Mate to make sure she shows, no one told her."

Dylan shook his head. He wasn't going to micromanage Zelda. It hadn't worked before and at this point, forcing her to stay with him was just guaranteeing trouble for everyone. And she had been there with him when they told the Council. If she had wanted to leave after the Raoul debacle, he had no doubt she would've.

He finally saw a group of wolves with graying fur emerge from the forest in the distance. They were here.

Edon came over and looked out the window before turning his attention to him. "Ready to make it official?"

He nodded. He'd been ready since the very beginning.

ZELDA LOOKED AT HERSELF IN THE MIRROR. SHE wore the white dress Annabelle had picked out for her and some sandals. It was simple and summery and probably would have been what she wore on her first date with Dylan if they had met in a normal way and had the time for that. It was kind of a shame that the dress would be ripped to shreds so soon. The Ritual happened in wolf form and the outfit was mostly an adaptation of a mortal wedding. Though given werewolves had been around much longer than modern weddings, it was more accurate to say it was the other way around.

The clock said that it was almost time to go back to the lake for the Ritual. She brushed out her hair one last time and went downstairs. She glanced around and didn't see Dylan inside the house.

Tasha and Tate smiled at her, and she was glad for it. She needed some positivity going into this life-changing moment.

She found the Council, Marcus, and Dylan waiting by the lake. He was still in human form, wearing a white button-down and black pants, standing next to the group of Elders. She knew the Ritual wasn't the same as a werewolf wedding, and it didn't resemble those held by humans, but she still felt a tug in her chest at the sight of him. It still felt like he was waiting at the altar for her. And instead of running away, she could barely wait to reach him. When she finally did, she took her spot next to him and listened to the Elders describe what was about to happen.

At their command, both she and Dylan Shifted. They stared into each other's eyes for a moment before one of the Elders cleared his throat, prompting them to proceed. Tradition stupidly said that the female had to be on her back, but her Mate surprised her when he lay down first.

Though she appreciated his gesture that proved he was on her side, it was still awkward to stand over him and place her jaw at his jugular. Especially after she'd already attacked him. She expected him to flinch, but he didn't. She wondered how he could still trust her so deeply after everything that had happened between them, but she was glad for it.

The feeling of his breath and his teeth against her neck brought her back to the present. He applied a little more pressure but didn't break the skin. Like he was asking if she was okay. She did the same and soon they were both biting each other hard enough to draw blood as required for the Ritual. Werewolves had venom which could kill vampires and turn humans. An Alpha bite could kill a normal werewolf, and the only way to not die would be to submit before it got too bad. Mates bit each other and the venom would mix with the other's blood until their scents fused. It Marked them as the other's property. She expected some shock at knowing she'd forever be Dylan's, but none came. If anything, she felt peace. And the excitement she felt at him being hers was overwhelming.

Can you hear me?

It was somehow different than when they'd communicated before. When they'd first met near the river, it felt as if they were talking on the phone. Now, it felt as if he were a part of her as much as her inner thoughts were. Hearing him in her mind was now as easy as breathing.

Before she could answer, fire raced through her veins and she started to get light-headed. It wasn't like when Raoul attacked her, although she was still his Alpha, so his venom didn't hurt her. But why would her Mate's bite hurt so much?

She heard Dylan calling her name again. This time, much more urgently. *Zelda, are you okay? Zelda! Answer me!*

But she couldn't. The only thing she could do was listen. Her jaw went slack, releasing Dylan and he did the same.

She couldn't hear him clearly anymore, but she had the feeling he was still trying to talk to her through the Bond.

Zelda felt something wet nudging her head and she knew it had to be her Mate's nose, but she couldn't open her eyes to confirm her suspicion. Every nerve ending was now on fire and what had started as an already painful experience was somehow getting even worse with every passing second.

Everyone knew the dangers of jumping into the Ritual too soon. But she thought that they were on the same page now. He'd been consistent this whole time, and she'd finally wanted it as much as him. *Why did it feel like she was dying?*

She couldn't hold in the pained whimper that escaped her. She saw Dylan Shift. She did the same, but it hurt more than usual.

She saw the men looking down at her and suddenly it all became too much. The pain hit her again and she saw a white light before everything faded out.

CHAPTER 14

DYLAN GROWLED AT ELDER KAI. HE HATED ANYONE seeing Zelda when she was vulnerable.

She had Shifted back to human form without clothes and he was doing his best to shield her from the men. He stayed in wolf form, ready to attack anyone who dared to come too close.

Aside from their physical audience, Dylan had the same sense that they were being watched from the trees. Or, even weirder, that the trees *themselves* were spying on him and Zelda. Although how or why that would happen, he had no idea. Aside from Raoul and his group of traitors, the Morsure Pack had no enemies and his Mate hadn't mentioned the Waya Pack coming after hers.

Dylan, his father said. He expected to be reprimanded, but it didn't come. He turned his head and saw him holding out a blanket. Dylan couldn't remember him leaving to get one.

He grabbed it in his jaws and draped it over Zelda. He could finally breathe easier, but he didn't stop guarding her. He'd felt their mental Bond forming before it was ripped away. Hearing her voice in his head had felt like a missing piece clicking into place.

You need to calm down, Elder Kai's voice admonished.

He took a deep breath. *Do not snap at the Council*, he reminded himself. It would only make everything worse. For him, Zelda, and their Packs. The Ritual failing meant none of them had security anymore.

Give her to me, he finally said, addressing his father. He stared at Marcus until he nodded.

Dylan knelt down so Marcus could easily and gently transfer Zelda to his back.

Dylan started to slowly walk back to the house, keeping his pace as steady as possible and his movements smooth so as not to jostle her any more than necessary. It would take much longer, but he didn't think his Mate would be able to handle another Shift on top of whatever agony she was going through.

He heard the Council follow, but he kept focusing on putting one paw in front of the other. He needed to put Zelda into bed and make sure she was okay before he could even think about dealing with the logistical and bureaucratic nightmare that was just starting.

Tasha and Tate were waiting for them at the door.

"What happened?" Tate demanded.

Tasha took a tentative step forward, and he knelt on the ground. He just stared at them, silently willing them to take Zelda.

They took the hint, draping his Mate's arms over their shoulders and helped her up the stairs.

Dylan could see her muscles shaking and it made him want to rip his hair out. He ran around back and Shifted. *Edon, meet me in Zelda's room. Bring Annabelle and your parents.*

Dylan ran upstairs and past the Council who were waiting outside his Mate's room. He opened Zelda's door and sat next to her on the bed. The twins, who were standing at the foot of the bed, had covered her in the blanket. Despite that, Zelda was still shivering.

"Thank you," he said to them.

He lifted his eyes toward the door, grateful that none of the Elders had presumed permission to enter. He might have done something irrational had they just barged in. He nodded at them and they filed in. Edon came in, holding Annabelle's hand while Connor and Esme brought up the rear.

They all took in the sight and he could see the different combinations of confusion and worry play across their features.

"Is she okay?" Annabelle asked.

Edon shook his head and she went pale.

No one was sitting except him and it made him feel like a lab rat being studied.

"Everyone, please take a seat."

The twins and his Pack, save his father, all immediately sat on the ground. The Elders glanced around and upon noting the lack of chairs in the room, didn't move.

Dylan held in a growl. He wasn't Alpha, and now he probably wouldn't be allowed to become one, but they could at least respect his wishes while his Mate was in distress.

Elder Kai cleared his throat. "You need to tell us what happened, Dylan. And speak to what Zelda was experiencing as much as possible as she is unable to answer our questions herself."

"Everything was going fine. Our Bond was forming, and then it suddenly went silent. I couldn't hear her anymore. *Alpha Makris*," he said, hating that the Council had called her by her first name, "released me, and I did the same once I realized she was in pain. Then she started shaking. You all heard her. You know as much as I do after that. But her being in pain—that's not normal."

"No, it's not. Although, it can happen when one or both wolves aren't fully committed."

"I don't think that was it." He couldn't believe that was the issue. Zelda was stubborn, but would she really risk her own life for her Pack? Who was he kidding? She probably would. He'd do the same in a heartbeat. "If it was, wouldn't we both be in pain?"

"Usually, the one who isn't fully committed has some resistance to the process and is therefore not fully neutralizing the other's venom."

This sounded way too similar to what Ivy had told him Fawn went through while she was in Hell. But in that case, Caleb had also been suffering. Why wasn't he? It was so rare for a Ritual to go wrong in the first place, he'd never thought much about it before Zelda had asked him to keep their status a secret.

"It would have been an immediate reaction," Elder Raghnall interjected. "There would have been no time for you to experience a mental Bond at all."

He'd never been so relieved to hear the know-it-all speak. It meant Zelda hadn't forced herself to go through with the Ritual just for her Pack's sake. But it also meant that something else had gone wrong. Something that seemed was a mystery to everyone in the room.

Which meant he had no way of combating it or curing Zelda.

"Unfortunately," Elder Raghnall continued, "because the Ritual failed, Zelda and the Equinox Pack are still considered Rogues. And neither of you can claim the title of Alpha until you've successfully completed the Ritual. You have until the end of next week to remedy the situation."

Dylan tamped down the irritation he felt at the declaration. He knew it was coming, but it wasn't a priority right now. The Elder's pre-occupation with the legislative fallout of the afternoon's events over Zelda's life chafed and pissed him off.

Dylan saw his father make eye contact with Connor and Elder Kai before he stood up and walked out of the room.

The adults quickly followed suit. Elder Kai the last of them, staying a few more moments to look at Zelda. Dylan swore he heard the man mutter something about "sins of the father" on his way out.

Dylan stared at the empty doorway. *What on earth was he talking about?* he asked Edon.

His Beta shrugged in response.

He pushed his hearing outside the room.

"I'd offer you the guest house, but it's currently occupied," Marcus said. "If you'd like, I'd be happy to pay for hotel rooms."

"That will be acceptable, Alpha Stone," Elder Raghnall replied.

Dylan pulled his hearing back in and turned to the remaining audience. "Could you make sure that Zelda's okay? I need to think through this."

A chorus of affirmations sounded.

He tilted his head toward the door and Edon followed him back into his room.

"Did you see that back there?" he asked.

"Your Mate lying ill in bed? Yeah. It was kind of hard to miss."

"Edon—" he growled.

"I'm not making a joke, Dylan." His tone was serious and he knew his friend was telling the truth. "What are you asking if I noticed if it's not that?"

"My dad knows something. And I think yours does, too." He didn't even care if his father heard him right now. His father knew something, and he needed to know what. It obviously had to do with Zelda and if he was lucky, it would save her.

"I can ask him—"

No. My dad clearly doesn't want me to know. I have one of his journals, so maybe that'll have something in it. I need you to help me read through the others.

Whatever you need.

He needed answers. And time. But he'd focus on the one he could control and hope it was enough to save his Mate. He'd just found her. He couldn't lose her now.

ZELDA SAW THE JAWS OPENING MOMENTS BEFORE SHE was hurtled into darkness as she was devoured whole.

She woke with a start, her eyes flying open to dispel the disturbing nightmare. Then she groaned and immediately closed her eyes again.

She could only stare at the backs of her eyelids. It was still too painful to open her eyes, but now the trouble was only in her head and chest. Her skull felt like it was being crushed from every angle and a tight band gripped her heart, giving no hint of letting up. Luckily, her blood had stopped flaming and she was now in control of her muscles again. Even if she were fully normal again, she didn't think her Pack members would allow her out of bed. They were all hovering over her as if she were about to die.

Maybe she was. She'd heard about the horrors associated with them, but she'd never suffered from bad headaches or migraines before. But even she couldn't imagine people dealing with this pain more than once in their life.

She heard Tasha and Tate bickering in the corner. They'd stopped briefly when they helped feed her food that Esme had brought up, but the truce hadn't lasted long.

It reminded her of how she used to be with Liekos. Before he'd become Alpha and unpredictably irritable. Before then, they'd never had a *bad* relationship. It was a normal one where the older brother constantly teased his little sister and she would throw it right back at him.

She hadn't thought of that side of him in so long. It was hard to when it was his bad decisions that had completely turned her life upside down. But she wasn't as angry at him as she used to be. If it hadn't been for him, she probably never would have met her Mate. Or learned what a loose cannon Raoul was.

She should have seen it sooner. She winced at the memory of him showing his true colors.

Immediately, the twins stopped arguing.

"Are you okay?" Tasha asked, mistaking her reaction as one to physical pain instead of emotional turmoil.

"Fine," she mumbled. "Has he come in again?" She hadn't been able to respond to any of it, but she was fully and acutely aware of Dylan's presence when he'd been in the room. His body heat had enveloped her, trying to balance out the freezing chill she'd been plagued with when he'd been protecting her in the clearing and in the bedroom while he grilled the Council for answers.

The men hadn't been helpful at all, and even if her Mate found out his father's secrets, it was still no guarantee to fix their situation. She doubted Marcus would have kept something so big to himself. He struck her as someone who would promptly report anything and everything to the Council.

In the meantime, she needed to fill her time. But everything she'd been thinking about lately, mainly Dylan and finding a home for her Pack, were both derailed by the Ritual failing. This wasn't an enemy she could fight. If it was, she'd already lost the fight without ever hearing the starting bell. Which left her with nothing to do but mope. But she refused to throw in the towel that easily. If only she could keep her eyes open long enough to sit up. Or do *anything*.

D YLAN WAITED OUTSIDE HIS FATHER'S OFFICE WHERE MARCUS and Connor were having a silent conversation he had no hopes of eavesdropping on. He'd almost gone in to grab another journal when he'd heard them enter through the secret entrance he'd discovered as a kid. While hiding out like a common thief, he'd read through the rest of the journal he had and it had finished without revealing any secrets. Although he was now scarred for life. He knew his parents had loved each other, but he didn't need to know *how* much. Or often. He shuddered and focused on the task at hand.

Connor had left a little while ago and shown no signs of returning soon. His shoulders had been tight and it looked as if he'd had an argument with his dad. If he'd sensed him, he hadn't alerted Marcus.

With the Ritual's failure, the feast for the Council had been canceled. He was glad. There's no way he could force that rich food down his throat while Zelda was still bed-bound. He'd had Esme bring her food, but he hadn't gone to see his Mate again since Elder Kai had confirmed that there was nothing that he or any of the other Elders could do for them.

He was about to go to the kitchen to pass the time when he heard his father's voice get loud.

"Stella! Look, I know you told me not to call you again after we talked a few weeks ago."

Was that why his father had suddenly taken a sabbatical? Because they'd had a fight? What was so bad that Stella would cut off communication with his dad?

"You have every right to be mad at me, but Dylan really needs you." There was a pause. "I was wrong to use you, but I swear, it only started that way. I really do consider you a friend. And I never forced him to befriend Alec or Fawn. Our kids bonded organically. We've all been friends for years, Stella. That has to count for something."

Dylan extended his wolf senses to hear Stella's response.

"It does to me. But I don't know if it does to you. You tricked me into casting a spell that kept him from finding his Mate before you moved back to New Orleans. And now that he has, you want me to help you again?"

She'd done *what*? Stella, who always talked about the importance of Fate and letting it run its course? And at his father's request?

"Honestly, Marcus, I would have done anything to help him had you just been honest with me from the beginning. I know what it's like to lose your soulmate too early, and I wouldn't wish that on anyone. I would have tried to help you break the curse no questions asked."

What curse? What was she talking about? And what did she mean about *losing your soulmate too early*?

"Don't you still care about him?" his father demanded.

"Don't take that tone with me."

He'd only heard Stella sound that stern once. And it had been when Fawn had once sneaked out to meet him in Central Park for a night-time walk a few days before the full moon. He'd never made that mistake again.

"Of course, I care about him," Stella continued. "He's like another son to me. But I'm not going to compromise my integrity again. I never should have cast that spell for you. This is Fate, Marcus. Even if I had willingly agreed and done it, this probably still would have happened. You have to deal with the consequences. And unfortunately, yet again, it seems Dylan will be affected by you not learning your lesson the first time."

"So, you won't help him. Or her."

There was a pause. "From what you described she should recover on her own. I sincerely hope Dylan and Zelda succeed. But you can't call me again to fix a problem for you. I mean it, Marcus. Just don't."

The call ended and Dylan sat silently around the corner from the closed doors. What had just happened?

She had given him a clue. Magic had something to do with it all. The problem was he didn't know anything about it. Had his father just lost him the most powerful ally he had against a problem he still couldn't fully define?

ZELDA'S STOMACH GROWLED, AND IMMEDIATELY ANNA WAS AT her bedside, having replaced the twins around dinnertime. She was grateful to their attentiveness, but she wanted privacy. Something that Dylan had apparently decreed impossible because once they left, Anna had taken their place without budging.

How she had ever thought Edon's Mate was timid was a mystery. The woman had steel in her spine when push came to shove.

It no longer hurt to have her eyes open, and now she only felt as if she had a really bad head cold. Her head was full of cotton, not pain anymore. She had no idea what had changed. Maybe Dylan had worked a miracle, but all she knew was that she wanted some privacy. She sat up and Anna surprisingly didn't insist she lie back down.

"You're doing better."

"Finally." She didn't know if she would have lasted until morning if it hadn't gotten better. She would never complain about the pain of Shifting again.

"I'm going to take a bath. You don't need to chaperone me."

"I'll stay out here. But if something feels wrong you have to tell me. I can't let my Luna down."

"I'm not your Luna."

"You are. It's just a technicality that the Council won't grant you the title." Anna rolled her eyes and Zelda was glad to know she wasn't the only one annoyed at the men who were in charge of all the were-wolves in the United States. "Once you're dry, I can go downstairs and get you more food."

She didn't answer and stepped into the bathroom. She turned on the tub and waited, sighing when she finally submerged herself in the hot water. It was as if she could immediately feel her stress melting away. She might have to start taking more baths.

Zelda wondered what Dylan was doing. She'd heard Marcus shout something downstairs a bit ago, but she hadn't been able to hear much more than that. Her hearing wasn't quite as sharp as it usually was. A nasty side effect of whatever was affecting her. She hoped all her senses returned to normal soon. Being unable to know what was happening sucked.

And her Mate clearly wasn't going to tell her until he believed she was healthy again. Once she was one hundred percent and could convince him to do away with the babysitters, she'd start making sure he was okay like he always did for her. She'd been selfish since they met, but no more.

They might not be officially Mated yet, but the best relationships were partnerships. She wasn't going to run or hide anymore. Her home was with him and the Morsure Pack, and she'd prove that she was as committed to them as him.

The question was how.

CHAPTER 15

DYLAN REREAD THE PAGE. HAD HE FOUND HIS father's secret? Elder Kai hadn't been exaggerating. *Sins of the father*, indeed. At least, according to the witches.

He'd been wrong. Or, at least partially mistaken. The secret wasn't about him and Zelda. Not directly.

And it also affected Edon. While his Beta hadn't known the whole back story, Connor must have.

Dylan turned the book around and shoved it under Edon's nose. He watched his friend scan the pages and the shock work its way across his features.

"Dylan, I had no idea—So, my dad..."

"Wasn't originally Beta."

"Because Zelda's dad was. Why did my dad never tell me?"

Probably because Marcus demanded his silence. If Dylan hadn't read all the details himself, he would still wonder what other secrets his dad was keeping from him.

His father had picked a fight after a Rogue had hit on his mom. It turned bloody in the St. Louis Cemetery, and a human cleaning off a witch's headstone had unwittingly trapped her in Limbo. In retaliation, the Quarter witches had placed a blood curse on both Marcus and Zelda's dad. They, and all their descendants, would lose their Mates and suffer the constant emptiness their sister feels in the afterlife.

How his dad could have ever become friends with Stella, no matter how nice she was, after that ordeal, he had no idea. If he'd been in his dad's position, he would have avoided witches altogether.

"Okay. So, now we know why today went wrong," Edon said.

Dylan thought about it. His father had been unwilling to talk about this, so why hadn't he come storming in the moment he realized his journal was missing. He'd grabbed it from the office and while his dad didn't necessarily catalog every book in there, his journals were always near him. If he truly didn't want him to know, there were ways of stopping him. Why hadn't he used any of them?

The only explanation he could think of was that seeing Zelda in pain made the shame so bad that his father had decided to silently come clean. It still wasn't the type of honesty Marcus had taught him and always practiced, but it was better than actually being blocked at every turn.

"But we still don't know how to break the curse."

He thought about contacting Fawn but immediately dismissed the idea. But he could call Alec.

He glanced at the clock. It was five in the morning. Too late to call. He'd call as soon as Alec was awake.

He walked to Zelda's door and knocked.

"Come in."

He opened it slowly.

Zelda was now sitting up in bed. Anna was napping in the desk chair. Not quite the scene he expected to see. He'd assumed that Zelda would have kicked her out by now, but maybe Anna had put her foot down. Either way, she could go to Edon now.

He touched her arm and she blinked blearily up at him.

"Thanks, Anna."

She nodded and left. *She's doing much better*, she mentally added.

"Hey," he said, sitting next to Zelda. "I heard you're doing better."

She smiled. "Almost back to normal now. I don't know why, but I'm not complaining."

Stella had been right. Despite her declaration to his father, though, Dylan wondered if she'd secretly helped out.

"I have something to show you." And then he handed her his father's journal, the relevant pages saved with the ribbon bookmark.

TEN MINUTES LATER, ZELDA SET THE BOOK ASIDE and met her Mate's expectant stare.

"No wonder your father didn't want me around."

"Yeah. I'm sure he doesn't want me to go through what he did and lose my Mate."

She tilted her head. He was missing the more worrisome outcome for a father. "Dylan, both our dads were cursed so their kids would lose their Mates. There's a chance that you could die. And no parent ever wants to see that." She'd seen how destroyed some of the older wolves in her Pack were after their sons were killed by the Waya Pack's counterattack. That had been *before* Raoul's brother had brokered a deal with the Waya Pack to have a one-on-one battle between the Alphas. It was one of the few times that Liekos' Beta had stood up to him. And, quite frankly, it had been too little, too late.

Dylan hadn't responded but instinct told her it wasn't fear of losing his own life but losing *her*.

His hand came up, holding hers to his cheek, and she felt heat skitter up through her arm, pleasantly awakening her nerve endings for the first time all day. And it somehow felt much more intimate than when they'd done in the clearing that afternoon. The Ritual was the most intimate moment Mates could have, and yet this small touch made her feel more connected to him than the brief meeting of their souls before everything had gone wrong.

Zelda watched his eyes scan her face as if he were truly seeing her for the first time and taking the time to memorize her features. She took the opportunity to see the same. Because now that she knew they had a magical ax hanging over their heads, she was determined to make the most of the time they had together.

They hadn't completed the Ritual, but in her mind, they'd made the commitment and connection. Unfortunately, it still didn't confirm the safety of her Pack or Dylan's position as Alpha of his. She'd heard Dylan talking to a friend. Maybe he'd know a way to break the curse so she and Dylan could move on with their relationship without the Council getting in the way.

Surprisingly, she couldn't bring herself to be mad at the witches, or even her dad. Their fathers had made a bad mistake and had paid for it. But the Council refusing Dylan his birthright pissed her off. Hadn't he proved himself by now? Marcus had left him in charge, something that never would have been able to happen if the Elders didn't already have faith in his ability to lead.

She kept her voice level but couldn't look Dylan in the eye when she spoke next. "So, Edon's dad was Alpha while you were in a different state?"

"My father still had the final say on important matters. I guess you could say Connor was acting Alpha."

The idea of being so far from her Pack didn't sit well with her. She wondered if Dylan felt similarly. He had a life in New Orleans, but he also had had one in New York. Would he ever ask her to relocate closer to his friends? Would he follow in his father's footsteps and become a backseat driver to his Beta regarding Pack business?

She dismissed the idea. Her Mate made dinner for his whole Pack every single day. It was a clear indication that he wanted to be involved on a personal level with his Pack.

His other hand went to her waist and pulled her closer. "Whatever happens, we have each other now. We'll get through this."

She smiled at him.

His eyes dropped her lips, and her breath hitched.

"Can I kiss you?" he murmured.

She leaned forward, moving her hand from his cheek to curl around the back of his head. She pulled him in and pressed her mouth to his.

Her head cleared completely, and the urge to get closer to him seemed to take over her body.

Dylan deepened the kiss and growled low.

The sound vibrated through her body and it only made her more frantic to be with him.

But he pulled back. He rested his forehead against hers. "You have no idea how much I've wanted to do that."

She didn't know how true that was until he said it. But now that she'd finally kissed him, she never wanted to stop.

"You've been through a lot, Zelda. I don't want to rush this."

Hadn't they just talked about their potentially limited time together? And he wanted to pull the plug tonight?

"You're not." She shifted closer until her body was fully pressed against his.

His self-control must have already been slipping because when she went to kiss him again, a groan escaped. He was as into it as she was when their fingers tangled in each other's hair. His hand curled around her thigh, pulling her onto his lap.

She nipped his lower lip and he bit her back in turn.

If this is what just kissing was like with her Mate, she wondered what everything else would be like. And it was said that after the Ritual, being together became that much more pleasurable because you could experience the other's pleasure at the same time. She might combust if that were true. But for now, she'd just keep kissing him.

HE HADN'T GONE BACK TO HIS ROOM AFTER he'd come in to check on his Mate. He'd expected her to tell him to leave once he'd put the brakes on their passion. When she didn't, he also hadn't been sure how they'd spend an evening together without giving in to their desire.

But she'd fallen asleep very soon after, and he'd been left staring at the ceiling alone while he took deep breaths until he calmed down. He closed his eyes and had tried to force his mind to go blank. He needed to be alert tomorrow. But doing that only made his mind spin out of control with the same worries he'd had all day. It was only after his mind had exhausted itself that he'd fallen into a dreamless sleep.

Dylan turned and immediately sat upright. Zelda wasn't next to him and he couldn't hear her in the bathroom. He threw off the covers and checked his room. Then downstairs. And that's when he noticed his car was missing.

His Mate was gone.

CHAPTER 16

Zelda had no idea where she was. When Dylan had taken her to Café DuMonde, they were away from the epicenter of the action. Although it had drawn a crowd for being so famous.

When she'd stolen Dylan's car that morning, she'd planned on driving right to the cemetery where their fathers had fought the third wolf, but she somehow got lost after parking in an over-priced lot. The least she could do was make sure her Mate's ride stayed safe. It might be the only thing she could do because her plan to talk to the witches wouldn't happen if she couldn't *find* them.

She'd assumed they weren't in the multiple, obvious stores and shops dedicated to magic, fortune-telling, or voodoo. But maybe she had it the wrong way around. What if they were hiding in plain sight? She turned around and walked back toward the throng of people and followed the crowd moving up Bourbon Street.

She felt her scalp begin to tingle as she passed by a small spiritual store. Ignoring her instinct to run, Zelda walked through the doorway.

A purple tapestry hung on the wall. It featured a white design of concentric circles and symbols she could never hope to translate.

A woman not much older than her was working at a small glass counter which housed an array of crystals and large, decorative cards she'd never seen before.

"Can I help you?"

Zelda glanced up. "I'm not sure. I'm looking for—"

"I know who you are. I don't know whether you're being here is brave or stupid. You're lucky to even—"

She cut herself off when another, older woman walked out from the back.

"Zelda Makris, how nice to meet you."

Was it? She didn't seem insincere, but then again, these women were the witches she'd been searching for. Members of the coven that had cursed her and Dylan as collateral damage.

"How can we help you?"

"I would like you to lift the curse on me and my Mate and our family line."

The woman smiled. "There's something to be said for straight-forwardness. Unfortunately, I can't do that."

"Why not? Your coven cast it."

"We're not as strong as we were then. We channeled the last of our ancestors' magic that lingered before your father trapped them in the demimonde."

"Demimonde?" She knew it was French, but she'd taken Spanish in school when it came time to choose a foreign language.

"The half-world between life and death," the younger witch interjected, disdain clear in her tone. Zelda expected her to roll her eyes to complete the attitude, but she didn't.

"They were pulled out of the peaceful afterlife, and we can no longer connect to them," the older woman explained. She shot a quelling glance at her companion, dismissing the other witch from the room. "The Lifting of the Veil spell from the Belgrave Grimoire will let us return our ancestors to their rightful place in the afterlife."

"What is that?"

"The most powerful spellbook in existence."

"And you want me to get it for you?"

The elder woman nodded. "We also need a vial of blood from the head vampire in the Quarter Clan and the voodoo idol statue stored in St. Louis Cathedral. And then we can lift the curse."

"But *will* you?" She wasn't about to be loopholed by these witches.

The woman paused, tilting her head to the side.

Zelda's spine straightened as she was scrutinized.

The woman made a sound of approval. "Yes. We will."

Zelda nodded. "How do I find these items?"

Instead of an answer, the woman grabbed her forehead, and panic kicked in. An image of an apartment building flashed across the inside of her eyelids. She instinctively knew it was located in New York. It shifted into a page with multiple circular symbols before that melted away into another building filling an entire block in New Orleans.

She now knew where to find the items, but how was she supposed to find a tiny statue in a giant church?

Responding to her thoughts, the woman said, "We do not know where it is hidden."

"Can—" Zelda tested her voice. "Can I ask why no one from your coven can get these?"

"We have a truce with the vampires where we leave each other alone. And the church is protected by a spell against witches."

What on earth?

The woman didn't elaborate. "No one must know of our deal."

"I promise, I'll keep it a secret."

"I guarantee it." With that bizarre pronouncement, she finally released Zelda and disappeared into the back of the shop.

Zelda felt a quick wave of dizziness and then it dissipated. Once she felt grounded again, she walked outside and back to the car. She had their word that they'd lift the curse. The problem was how on earth she was going to find a spellbook she'd never seen before the deadline passed and Dylan had to throw her and her Pack out?

DYLAN GLANCED AT THE CLOCK. ZELDA STILL HADN'T returned and he couldn't take it anymore. It was still early, only seven in the morning, but it was time to call for help.

"Hello?" Alec whispered.

"Alec? Hey, did I wake you up?"

"No, no, I'm up."

He felt like an ass. His friend had obviously been sleeping.

"What's up with you?" Alec asked.

"I wish I could say it was smooth sailing, but I actually have a favor to ask you."

"Sure, what is it?"

"There's a coven of witches in New Orleans that's posing a bit of a problem for my Pack." Now, he just had to tell him about Zelda. He cleared his throat. "They cursed my soulmate a while back—" It wasn't the whole truth, but it was close enough.

He didn't get to finish before Alec cut in.

"Wait, your soulmate?"

Yeah, he knew that would require a more in-depth explanation. He'd do it once he could see Alec in person. "Long story. Anyway, would you be able to come down here to..." To what, exactly? Step in because your mom is letting my Mate suffer because she's pissed at my dad? "I don't know, convince them to be nice?"

All witches were on good terms with each other, right? And the Quarter witches had helped them all fight the demon invasion and Lucifer back then. He hoped that alliance was still good.

"My dad and I have tried every bargaining trick we can think of and they just won't lift the curse." Not quite true, but his dad had pleaded a lot with Stella and the journal had detailed Marcus begging the witches for forgiveness right after they cursed him. It obviously hadn't worked.

"Um, my mom might be better equipped to handle the situation."

"Yeah..." Did Alec not know? "Between you and me, my dad and your mom had an argument a few weeks ago, so I don't know if that's a good idea." It *absolutely* wasn't, but if he said that, he'd have more questions to answer.

"I mean, I can definitely come down, but I'll need more info. How soon do you need me down there?"

"By tomorrow, if possible? I'm sorry it's so last minute. I thought I could handle it but my soulmate may have pissed them off further." Somehow. What else would explain her going missing? He just hoped the curse hadn't already kicked in and she was gone for good. "Who knows what would happen next? I don't want to find out."

"Speaking of soulmates, can I bring mine?"

"Of course, you can." He hadn't seen Ivy in forever. Not since she and Alec's wedding a few years ago. And he hadn't stayed long to chat. It was still uncomfortable for him to be around Fawn and Caleb and he hadn't wanted to spend more time with them than necessary. Which made him a shittier friend to Alec than he was to him. "But you might want to tell her that there's not a lot of parties for us wolves in the Quarter since the whole thing with the witches started." Now he knew why his dad never liked him staying there so late.

"I'll be sure to pass that on. See you soon."

Dylan could hear the smile in his friend's voice and couldn't help but also smile. "Thanks, Alec. You're a life-saver."

"No problem, man."

The call ended and he had a feeling it was because of Ivy.

Dylan heard tires rolling closer and glanced out the window. He felt every muscle in his body relax when he saw the car pull back into the backyard and park next to the truck.

His soulmate was back.

ZELDA HAD BARELY CLOSED THE DRIVER DOOR BEFORE Dylan was pulling her into a hug.

He buried his face in her neck and merely inhaled. "I thought you were gone," he murmured against her collarbone.

"I'm sorry. I just needed—" *to confront the witches.* What she said instead was, "some time to think."

What the hell? She hadn't meant to lie to him. *Why did she say that?* The witch had said she'd ensure she kept their meeting secret. Was this what she meant?

He looked up and scanned her face. "Did I move too fast?"

"No!" Too forceful. "No," she repeated, softer this time. "Not at all. I don't regret anything about that, Dylan."

"You're not going to leave?"

"No. I'll stay as long as you'll have me." Or until the Council forced her out.

"I called a friend to help. He should be arriving tomorrow."

That grabbed her attention. Who outside the Pack would be so trustworthy and dependable to come on such short notice? "What's his name?"

"Alec Belgrave."

She remembered hearing that before, but she got stuck on the *last* name. She forced herself to casually ask, "How can he help?"

"He's a witch."

So, he *was* related to the spellbook. Maybe getting it wouldn't be so hard, after all.

Dylan kept talking. "And his soulmate is accompanying him. I was really close friends with both of them when my dad moved us to New York after my mother was killed."

"What is he like?"

"Well, he's probably too snarky for his own good, and is one of the best men I've ever known."

"And his soulmate?"

He smiled. "I think I'll let you meet Ivy on your own. You'll get a good sense of her almost immediately."

"Will I like her?"

"I think so. It might be a mistake introducing you to each other. Together, you could take me and Alec down easily."

Zelda tried to picture who Ivy could be. She wondered what being friends with, much less being the soulmate of someone with magical powers. And what type of magical powers? She'd never given much thought to whether witches were real. The most she'd ever thought of them was when she saw them in movies and TV. And none of those were ever consistent with each other.

She swallowed her curiosity. She'd get answers soon enough. Even if he failed to actively break the curse, she was now confident Alec would help. He just wouldn't know it until after the curse was lifted.

CHAPTER 17

LUNCH AND THE REST OF THE DAY PASSED without any problems, but Dylan found himself still expecting something else to go wrong. He kept an eye on Zelda and stayed as close to her as possible.

He was pleasantly surprised when Zelda pulled him into her room when it was time to go to bed. One day soon he wanted her in his bed instead of the guest room, but he wouldn't pass up the opportunities afforded him in the meantime.

Alec hadn't gotten back in touch, so he didn't know the specific details of when his friend was arriving. Knowing his friend, however, he probably took the first flight available because he'd asked him to come as soon as possible. He wasn't one to take things too literally, but when it came to having each other's back, he and Alec had always gone above and beyond for each other.

The next morning, Dylan turned and saw Zelda's hair laid out on the pillow beside him. Quietly, he moved his arm from her waist and lifted his side of the blankets. His hand was on the door when he heard her move.

"Dylan?"

Her voice was still husky with sleep and he wished he could climb back under the covers with her and let Alec find his way to the compound on his own. But that was impossible and would make him a shitty host. "Just going to go get ready for the day," he murmured.

She nodded and lay back down, facing the door this time.

He showered, changed, and grabbed his phone before returning to his sleepy Mate. There was one new text message from Alec. His flight was landing soon. Shit.

"I need to go to the airport. Do you want to come with me?"

He could see the sleep still clouding her golden eyes.

She rubbed a hand over her face and yawned. "Right now?"

"Yes. Alec should be arriving any moment now. It's fine if you want to take more time to get ready. I'm bringing them right back and they'll probably have breakfast with everyone. I just didn't want you to wake up to an empty bed and wonder where I'd gone."

She smiled tiredly. "Thank you."

He leaned forward and kissed her forehead. "I'll see you soon."

When he pulled up to the Arrivals terminal, he parked the truck and waited for Alec and Ivy to emerge.

He spotted Ivy first. Even if he didn't know her, it would be hard to miss the large, bright blue suitcase Alec was lugging behind her. He bit his lip to keep from smiling. Strangers would assume she had forced him into playing the bellboy, but he knew that his friend had probably insisted.

He held his arms out wide.

When she finally made it to him, she hugged him. And almost immediately stepped back. "Ugh, you're sweaty."

He smiled. "It's summer, city princess. Get used to it out here." It had been a bit of an adjustment when he'd returned from New York, but this was definitely his home.

She stuck her tongue out and he felt like they were back in elementary school all over again. She glanced around and he could see the gears turning in her head. "Where is this soulmate of yours anyway?"

"She's back at the house. You'll meet her soon enough, but don't scare her off." He was joking. Zelda's instinct to run had clearly passed after yesterday. She'd reassured him so many times that that morning hadn't been her leaving him. And he'd never been more relieved.

"If she's worth it, she won't be intimidated by me. Just please tell me it's not Bailey."

He couldn't help grinning at that. "No, it's not. But you may see her since she's still in the Pack."

Ivy rolled her eyes. "Ugh. Don't remind me."

He just hoped they wouldn't jump at each other's throats again.

Alec arrived and let go of the suitcases to hug Ivy from behind. "Hey, man. Mind helping me get these in the trunk?"

"No problem." He grabbed them and easily brought them to the back of his truck. He waved his foot underneath the bumper and the back opened so he could slide them into the bed. He shut it and opened the door for Ivy. She climbed in, and before he could open the passenger door for Alec, his friend climbed in after her.

He moved to the front.

"Nice leg room," Alec said.

"It has to be. Werewolves aren't exactly small." Dylan buckled his seatbelt and pulled away from the curb.

"No kidding," Ivy half-laughed.

Twenty minutes into the drive, Dylan glanced in the rearview mirror and saw Ivy's eyes regularly fluttering shut. Alec quickly became her pillow as she napped.

Dylan briefly caught his friend up to speed and soon after even as a fellow morning person, his friend also napped. He couldn't blame them. Their flight had required them to get up much earlier than normal and he made a note to treat them a night on the town once everything was resolved.

Dylan gently pulled to a stop outside his home and put the truck in park. He climbed out and pulled their suitcases into the home and put them in his room. Then he remade the bed with new sheets and cleaned up. He went back outside and saw they were still sleeping.

He knocked on their window and waited for them to climb out.

"Welcome to the home of the Morsure Pack."

Z ELDA LOOKED THROUGH HER BEDROOM WINDOW AT THE couple chatting with Dylan. He grabbed their suitcases and walked inside.

"I'm going to put you in my room. Just give me some time to tidy up. There's food in the fridge," her Mate was explaining.

She could hear the guests' stomachs growl at that, but the girl said, "Stop stalling, Dylan. We want to meet her already."

Was she supposed to meet them down there?

She opened her door and saw Dylan walk into his room. She followed and watched him put his discarded clothes away. When he stripped the bed and pulled out new bedding, she said, "Want help?"

"Sure."

They completed the task in moments and soon his bedroom looked clean enough to be in a hotel. "So, you'll be staying in my room for a while?" she asked.

He met her curious gaze. "I can sleep on the floor if you want."

She took a deep breath. "No. You don't have to do that."

He led her downstairs. "I want you to meet my childhood friends, Alec and Ivy."

Zelda smiled and held out her hand to each of them. When Ivy shook hers, the smell of the ocean hit her. What was that?

"I know that look." Ivy smiled. "It just means I'm a siren."

"What?"

"I smell like the ocean to werewolves. It's not a big deal."

How did she know what a werewolf thought she smelled like? Had Dylan told her? And if she were a siren, did that mean that any man near her was at risk of falling under some hypnotic spell?

Her Mate walked away and into the kitchen. "I'll be right back."

Once he was out of sight, the guy named Alec wasted no time and asked, "How long have you been staying here?"

"Oh, just a few days."

"So, you just moved in?"

Zelda nodded. How much had Dylan told them?

If he told them about the Raoul debacle, she couldn't blame his friends for not welcoming her with open arms. She'd hurt Dylan. She didn't know if she'd ever stop feeling guilty for that. Or if she deserved to get over it at all.

Her Mate didn't seem to notice. He walked back into the living room and handed Alec a beer bottle and a soda for Ivy. "I can show you my dad's journal if you need it."

"Dylan."

Zelda flinched and turned around to see Marcus standing in the back door of the kitchen. "Can I talk to you?"

Her Mate placed a hand around her waist and stepped beside her, facing the new addition.

She held her breath as everyone watched Alpha Stone.

"I'm busy right now, Dad."

Zelda could feel the temperature of the drop and it was all she could do not to run away.

Alec's expression only confirmed what she already knew. She'd only recently met both Stone men, but even she could tell that it was a big deal for Dylan to brush off his father.

She was relieved when they all moved away from the situation and into Dylan's bedroom.

He let them all go in first, and then he closed the door.

His friend sat down in the desk chair and Ivy sat on the bench at the foot of the bed.

Zelda glanced around. Should she sit next to Ivy? Or on the bed? Where was Dylan going to sit?

Her Mate made the choice for her when he grabbed her hand and led her to sit next to him on the bed. He wrapped his arm around her waist, pulling her into him. She gave in to the warmth of his body and lay her head on his shoulder.

She didn't miss Alec's raised eyebrow. Ivy had a similar reaction.

Either oblivious, but more likely ignoring his friends' reaction, Dylan said, "Please tell me you know how to help us."

She practically felt Alec's sigh reverberate through the room. "I'll do my best. But you have to know that I don't use magic that much."

"He calls it an *unfair advantage* in life," Ivy added. She clearly didn't share the same opinion.

Zelda found herself agreeing with the siren. If she had magic, she'd definitely be able to solve a lot of problems nonmagical people couldn't. There was no way to claim magic wasn't a pass on life, but she also agreed that if she had that upper hand, she'd use it. If that made her a bad person then... it was what it was.

"Just because you're rusty doesn't mean you can't help. There has to be something in that giant Grimoire of yours."

A LEC GLANCED AT ZELDA BEFORE LOOKING BACK AT him. "I don't have the Grimoire with me."

Those were *not* the words he wanted to hear from his childhood best friend. He knew that there weren't life and death facing the Belgraves anymore, but surely they still used magic? Stella had her business and Fawn— he cut that thought off immediately.

"Then how can you do magic?" Zelda asked.

"Not all magic requires spells. They're normally reserved for more serious types of magic. My mom has the Grimoire for safekeeping."

"Wouldn't a curse qualify as Grimoire-worthy?" Zelda shot back. His Mate was clearly trying not to be as snarky as normal, but her wit still cut Alec's excuses to shreds. He was glad she was no longer antagonizing *him*, and that they were now on the same side.

Dylan saw Ivy's eyebrow tick up and bit back a smile. He could see respect for Zelda burgeoning in her assessing eyes. He hoped they would eventually become friends. But he hadn't missed Dylan and Ivy's initial disapproval of her. He knew they both had very good intuition but given that he hadn't actually mentioned anything that would have painted Zelda in a negative light. The problematic aspects of their relationship where *she* had been resistant were only known by him, her, Edon, and Annabelle. Though he suspected his dad, Connor, and Esme knew more than they let on. Even Bailey unfortunately knew the worst highlights. He definitely hadn't told Alec about her attacking him at the start of their relationship.

"Yes," Alec replied, tightly.

There would clearly be a lot more work before those two could be nice to each other.

Dylan cut in before the conversation devolved into a sniping match between his Mate and best friend. "Then what *can* you do?" Because as much as he was happy for his friend to finally see his home, now wasn't the time to be entertaining guests if there wasn't another reason for them to be here.

"I'll try to break the curse." Alec sounded affronted by the insinuation that he wouldn't. "But I don't want you to get your hopes up. Dylan knows that my mom and sister are more experienced at this stuff than I am."

He glared at Alec who had the good sense to look contrite for bringing up Fawn, even if only indirectly. Dylan closed his eyes and counted backward from five. His friend wasn't wrong but sharing that would only make Zelda curious about why he asked the least qualified witch he knew to handle the issue. Her fingers interlaced with his and she squeezed his hand tightly. He braced himself for her inevitable question, but it never came. Maybe she already knew. He hoped it didn't turn into another fight after they'd already covered and cleansed themselves of their past relationships.

"Why aren't they here with you?"

"My mom's a little mad at Marcus right now."

"And your sister?"

Alec glanced at Dylan, then answered, "I don't know."

Zelda sighed. "We'll take any help you can give."

Ivy whispered something to Alec, and it took all his self-control to not eavesdrop. His friend sighed. "I'll do my best."

Ivy smiled at both of them and Dylan felt a little bit of hope flare in his chest.

An hour later, Zelda stayed very still as Alec put some weird paste on her forehead like she was baby Simba in *The Lion King*. But he hadn't just swiped it across her skin. No, he'd finger-painted some symbol on her head that she couldn't mentally follow. It only gave her a headache. And that was separate from the stinging sensation that immediately skittered its way down her body as her nerve endings came to life. She then watched him do the same to Dylan, and it was only then that she could see the design of a tight cluster of straight lines and sharp angles.

Alec wiped his hand on a paper towel and then said, "both of you need to lie down with your heads touching and your feet pointing outward this way and that way." He gestured to the arms of the star within the pentagram drawn on the floor. It was adorned with even more symbols she didn't understand.

Her Mate had grumbled about ruining the wooden floor. Alec hadn't explained much of what was happening, but if he ended up summoning a demon to possess her, she'd go after him first.

He looked up from his notebook and frowned at her. "I can hear your thoughts, you know."

Crap. She wasn't used to any non-werewolf hearing her in human form.

Ivy didn't seem to know what was happening, so maybe it was only witches who could eavesdrop on unsuspecting people's thoughts? Either way, assuming this witchiness didn't kill her, she'd give him a piece of her mind.

"You're not hiding them at all." He still sounded grumpy, but now sounded more annoyed than genuinely offended.

"If you were a gentleman, you'd teach me how to do that."

"I'm here to lift a blood curse because you both have a deadline to meet, not give you a crash course on magic. Your Mate could have called my sister and her soulmate for that."

And now Alec was back to being a jerk. Why was he so hostile?

Dylan must have been thinking the same thing because she felt as much as she heard his growl rumble through the room.

Even Ivy glanced up in alarm.

Alec didn't seem to care. "This might hurt."

Which was what everyone wanted to hear while being the main subject of a magic ritual.

She could have sworn she saw the edge of his lip twitch. Couldn't this man pick an attitude and stick to it?

Without any warning, he began speaking. She couldn't recognize any of the words, but if she remembered her elementary school education correctly, he was speaking Latin as easily as if he communicated in the dead language on a regular basis. And he said he was *rusty*?

Pain exploded. Her blood begin to boil as if someone were trying to force her surrender by making her own body burn itself from the inside out. It was inescapable and exactly like what had happened with the Ritual.

This time, she heard Dylan grunting in pain and knew he was feeling it with her this time. She hoped Alec would end it soon, but he hadn't given a time estimate in how long this was supposed to take. The pain was enough to turn a single minute into an eternity.

It continued for who knows how long before it finally stopped. It didn't dissipate slowly but came to a complete halt. She lay panting on the ground, staring blankly at the ceiling, when Ivy's face and an outstretched hand came into view.

Zelda grabbed it and groaned as she was pulled into a sitting position. Her head still hurt and her stomach felt weighed down by a ton of bricks. Dylan was hunched over. She gently laid a hand on his back. He stiffened in surprise before he turned towards her, his pained gaze meeting hers. Sweat beaded on his forehead, and she felt awful knowing he had to go through the same torment as her.

"Did it work?" Ivy asked.

One glance at Alec was enough to dash any hopes she had.

She felt her Mate rest his head on her shoulder and knew she now had no other alternative than fulfilling her mission for the Quarter witches. Dylan had done all he could to save her. Now it was her turn.

part three

Remember that you are a wolf.
And you cannot be caged.

SARAH J. MAAS

CHAPTER 18

A S SOON AS THEY FINISHED SCRUBBING THEIR FOREHEADS and the floor clean, Dylan hunched over in an all-too-familiar posture. He was Shifting in the middle of the room. Without thinking, Zelda yanked the door open and pushed Ivy through, ignoring the siren's protests. Alec didn't look scared, but he didn't offer a fight when it came time for him to leave, too. Best friend or not, he must know that werewolves were dangerous during the Shift, even after years of becoming more aware and self-controlled in the process.

She watched helplessly as he was clearly forced into the painful transformation. She could feel the echo of his pain by the nature of being his Mate, but their failed Ritual didn't allow her to feel it fully.

How did that even happen? According to him, a spell on the house prevented Shifting inside, but he'd gone through the transformation like any werewolf would outside. The only difference was he'd done it involuntarily without a full moon.

Are you okay? she asked.

The moment his transformation finished, he whimpered and his panicked voice sounded in her mind. *I can't turn back.*

The only explanation she could think of was another trick of the Quarter witches. Had they placed the house spell in the first place? If it was them, she'd already promised to help them. Why were they punishing Dylan even more?

Zelda knelt down and placed a hand on his head. She gently stroked the fur between his ears. *I'm going to fix this.* When he didn't answer, she continued the motion until she felt his breathing even out. Only then did she stand and reopen the bedroom door.

Alec and Ivy jerked back, confirming her suspicion that they had had their ears pressed against the door the whole time. Behind them were also Edon and Annabelle. Without saying a word, she could see they also knew something was wrong. On the verge of tears, she grabbed both guys' hands and pulled them inside. Their soulmates followed and she shut the door behind them.

She knelt next to Dylan again, staring up at the people closest to her Mate. It made it all the much easier to do what she needed to. "He can't Shift back into a human."

Edon immediately glanced at Alec. "Can't you do something?"

He shook his head. "I could ask my sister, Fawn, but I don't know if she'd be able to help."

Fawn was his sister? The same Fawn that Dylan had dated? And she was a super-powerful witch? But Dylan hadn't called her to help? What did that mean? Did he not want her here because they weren't friends anymore? Or was it because he still cared about her? She believed Dylan that he'd washed her away during the Cleansing in the lake, but it wasn't as if that were an actual *spell.* It was only symbolic. And that meant it couldn't *actually* erase someone's feelings for someone in their past—

"I might be able to," Zelda said, forcing the words past the lump in her throat. If Alec couldn't fix the problem, and Fawn wasn't coming—for whatever reason—she needed to do all she could to help. "But I have to go away for a bit." She was telling the truth and apparently, she could say as much even with the witch forbidding her from sharing their deal.

Edon turned his attention her, his eyes narrowing.

"I don't know how long it'll take."

She'd never really had to think about how long it would take to get from one place to another in wolf form. Growing up, she'd lived on the Equinox Pack territory, and since her brother's death, she'd only been focused on moving the Pack to a new home, regardless of how long it took. If she ran in wolf form, it still might be too slow to get back in time for the witches to lift the curse before the Council's deadline. Maybe she could ask the Quarter witches, but that didn't feel right. They'd given her a task and maybe they'd consider it cheating if she used them to get it done. Besides, if she left right from the Morsure home in wolf form, she wouldn't have to deal with the human traffic of the city.

"I'll be back."

He didn't look like he believed her any more than before, but she didn't have time to give a big speech about why he could trust her now. She didn't even know if she *could* because the only thing that would likely convince him would be to talk about the deal she'd made with the Quarter witches, and despite them letting her talk in very general terms, she doubted they'd let her say anything close enough to the full truth to make a difference.

"Alec, can I trust you all to take care of him?"

He nodded, and she thought she saw a glimmer of respect in his eyes.

But once she got there, it should be easy. She'd seen the building where the Belgrave Grimoire was and all she had to do was look up directions. She expected Alec to react to her thoughts like he normally did, but his face showed no recognition of her inner monologue. The Quarter witch had also cloaked her thoughts regarding her mission.

"Do you need someone to go with you?" Ivy asked.

"No. But thank you for offering."

The siren nodded and eyed her with an intensity that made Zelda feel as if she could see through her. Did sirens have mind-reading powers? She'd never paid much attention to myths because she'd always thought werewolves were the only real magical creature normal humans talked about. She'd never thought about witches and sirens being real, so she had no idea what a siren could do. The one thing she assumed was true was they could somehow hypnotize all men that they were willing to jump overboard to their deaths if the Greek classics were to be believed.

When Ivy didn't say anything else, Zelda continued on.

"Edon," she said, "try to keep this from Marcus and the rest of the Pack." The fewer people knew about where she was going, the less she had to lie about what she was doing.

Her Mate's Beta no longer looked distrustful of her, but he didn't look happy. He winced like the words physically hurt him. "My mom is going to find out no matter what I do."

She hadn't thought about Esme, which was stupid, given she had first-hand experience with her uncanny ability to know when something was wrong. And she wasn't even a witch. It was a wonder that the woman hadn't already intruded on their group and discover her and Dylan mid-curse-breaking ritual or now since her Mate got trapped in wolf form.

Edon kept talking. "Can't I just tell my parents and Marcus? They are the Alpha and Beta of the Pack, and they're responsible for all of us. Including your Pack if you're leaving. If only temporarily." The last part was added skeptically, but he wasn't done. "If they asked me outright, I'd have to tell the truth anyway."

Zelda blew out a breath. "Fine." There really was no other way around it. "Just please take care of him. And I know our Packs aren't officially merged, but as I don't have a Beta anymore and people already know Dylan is my Mate, I'm naming you as my Beta and give you permission to govern the Equinox Pack in my absence. I'll be back as soon as possible. I promise."

She left before anyone could ask any more questions. In her room, she packed some necessities and draped the large strap over her neck. Silently walking down the stairs, she hoped she wouldn't run into someone on her way out. The moment she wished it, she expected life to do the exact opposite. But she got out of the home without anyone intercepting her. In the shadow of the house, she Shifted, her neck now fully filling the bag's strap. It would stay on while she ran to the French Quarter. Hopefully, the witches wouldn't trap her in wolf form, too.

It wasn't until she was at the edge of the clearing that she heard a wolf cry. Without completing the Ritual, there was a limit to how far her mental connection to Dylan could reach, but she knew it was him.

She forced herself to keep going instead of buckling to her instinct to rush back to him and comfort him. If she didn't complete the witch's mission and break the curse, they'd be separated permanently rather than only temporarily. And now that she'd found him and accepted him as her Mate, she wasn't going to let anything take him away from her.

D YLAN PROWLED AROUND HIS ROOM WHILE ALEC AND Ivy were whispering to Edon and Annabelle. He was stuck within the four walls for probably the same reason he was trapped in wolf form. Not that he wanted to be seen by his Pack members right now, but *not* having the option just made it worse. Luckily, no one would come in to see him either. He'd seen Alec cast a silencing spell on the room, so no one outside could hear what was happening. Their whispering was to keep him out of the loop, even though he could still hear what they were saying.

"You don't think she's running away, do you?" Ivy asked. "She seemed really eager to go off alone."

No! He expected Edon to look over given he'd mentally shouted, but there was no response at all. Then it hit him. The witches hadn't only trapped him in wolf form, but they had also taken away his ability to communicate with others. At least, anyone other than Zelda. And she wasn't here to translate or do anything else for him.

Focusing back on what Ivy was saying, he got pissed off all over again at her condemnation of Zelda's character. It sounded exactly like something Bailey would say, and if he were human, he'd point that out. He knew being associated with her would make Ivy immediately change her mind. But no matter how much he tried to communicate with Alec, Edon, or even Annabelle, he couldn't get through. But he wouldn't take anyone insulting Zelda, especially when she wasn't there to defend herself. So he growled low. Her startled gaze met his and she had the decency to look contrite.

"She's past that," Annabelle answered. "She wouldn't leave him, us, or her Pack behind without telling anyone but us. She's coming back."

The conviction in her voice made him happy to know Zelda had found another ally in his Pack. He'd supported her from the start, but she still didn't have many friends in the Morsure Pack. And his dad being against their union didn't help her cause since most of the older wolves followed his lead.

"What are we supposed to do in the meantime?"

"You can't try something else?" Edon asked.

"I haven't worked much on transformation spells. And I couldn't break the blood curse on them, so I doubt I'll do much better on a werewolf transformation curse." His tone was hard, and even without hearing Alec's private thoughts, Dylan knew that he was probably blaming himself for not being able to fix the problem. He and Fawn were perfectionists in everything, and he bet that extended to magic. Ivy gently touch him, and his tone softened. "I really wish I could do more, but my sister is more likely to help." He didn't even bring up his mom, and that was probably for the best given his father was back, but if they were both being perfectly honest, Stella was likely the best bet given she had more experience.

"Then call her," Edon said. "We need all the help we can get."

Alec pulled out his phone, but Ivy laid a hand on his, preventing him from calling.

"If Dylan wanted to, he would've already done it before this happened," Ivy said.

"The situation has changed," Edon argued.

"But we still should respect Dylan's decision," Annabelle interjected.

Both his male friends shared a look, and Dylan braced himself for what they were about to say.

"He was being stubborn," Alec said.

"I was going to say coward," Edon said.

Dylan bristled, but he couldn't say they were wrong either. He'd been avoiding Fawn for too long, and they really did need her help. More now than ever before.

"Just do it," his Beta urged, and Alec obliged.

He could hear Fawn's voice after the third ring. "Alec? It's 6 in the morning. This better be an emergency."

"You could've texted me you were in England."

"It was an impromptu trip last night. Now get to the point."

"I'm in New Orleans and Dylan needs your help."

"Is he okay!"

"If you could come down here—"

"I'll be there soon. Caleb—"

Dylan lay down. He didn't want to hear this part, but he heard Fawn and Caleb speaking. The angel didn't sound happy about cutting their trip short, but she wasn't budging, and he was grateful to have a friend like her. From now on, he'd be a better one to her.

ZELDA DIDN'T EVEN HAVE TO KNOCK BEFORE THE door to the witches' shop opened. "I need to get to New York quickly to complete your quest. It would take me almost three weeks to get there if I ran." And that was with enhanced werewolf abilities that allowed them to run fifty percent faster than a normal wolf.

She expected the woman to look surprised, but she just nodded in understanding. "Come into the back."

Zelda did, steeling herself for an ambush just in case. They walked through the store and behind a velvet curtain and she watched the witch grab the handle to what she assumed was a broom closet.

The woman muttered an incantation, then opened the door and gestured for her to walk in. "You'll have to find your own way back."

That would still be a problem, but at least it was still much better than having to run *both* ways. Zelda walked through the door and suddenly found herself standing in front of the giant, stone building she had seen in her vision. It looked like a mini-castle, and it only made her more anxious about infiltrating and stealing the Belgrave Grimoire. A building this fancy had to have security that would let Alec's mother she was there. She just needed a way to get alone with the book and a way to flee.

She walked into the lobby and was confronted with the doorman. "I'm here to visit the Belgraves?"

He didn't even look at her. "The elevator's that way. I've already programmed it to take you, all you have to do is ride it up."

Wow, that was fancy. A building where people didn't even have to push a button going up?

The doorman's complete indifference to her presence also made her feel better. Maybe accomplishing this mission would be easier than she thought. She entered the elevator and was surprised to see the button for the penthouse was lit up. Now the man's explanation made a lot more sense.

The metal door opened, and Zelda was surprised yet again because a dark-haired woman stood in the open door. She wore a knowing smile.

"Zelda, right?"

Well, shit. Why hadn't she thought of Alec's mom being psychic? Were the Quarter witches able to hide her mission from her, even if they apparently couldn't conceal her arrival?

"Yes... and you must be Ms. Belgrave?"

"You can call me Stella. Any friend of Dylan's is a friend of mine." The woman stepped aside, welcoming her inside. "It's so nice to finally meet you."

Did Alec tell her about her? But why would he have? It's not like he knew that she was headed to New York.

"I don't know what you know, but I have a bit of a problem." She wasn't magically stopped, so she kept talking. "Alec came down to New Orleans to help Dylan and me with something, but Dylan got trapped in wolf form and we don't know how to help him." A white lie. "I was wondering if you had a spell that could undo it? And given Alec is there, I could send him a picture of it."

Stella's eyes narrowed ever so slightly, examining her with such intensity that she was worried that even without magical intuition, the woman would know she was lying. She held her breath, praying her answer was enough for her to get the access she needed.

"Come right this way," she said.

This time, Zelda felt more at ease following a witch into a back room, but she was still nervous. Not because she was worried Stella would harm her or Dylan, but because of the potential consequences of being caught stealing and more importantly, failing to meet the Quarter witches' demands.

Stella pushed a large wooden door open, revealing a room with dark wood and rich colored fabric covering a small table and the windows. An ornate box lay on the table and Zelda stepped forward to examine it, unable to contain her curiosity.

Stella sat down on the far side of the table and gestured to the seat opposite her. "Before anything else, would you indulge me?"

What choice did she have? Zelda sat down, her anxiety kicked up another notch. If another werewolf were in the vicinity, they'd be able to hear her blood pumping through her veins. She just hoped witches weren't able to do the same.

Stella lifted the lid of the box and extracted a velvet pouch. From that, she pulled out a deck of cards. But they were larger and longer than any playing cards Zelda had ever seen. The backs were decorated with silver filigree over a purple background. The design reflected some light in a mesmerizing way that made it hard to look away.

Alec's mother swiped her hand across the deck, spreading them in an arc across the table. "Please pick a card."

Zelda immediately reached for one but hesitated with her hand in the air when Stella added, "Take your time. Let them speak to you."

Zelda closed her eyes and reopened them to scan the cards. She couldn't see what was on the other side of any of them, but her attention snagged on one towards the right end. Was she supposed to pick it up? She settled for touching the card and waited.

"You can flip it over."

She did so and saw a man in a black suit with piercing eyes. He was handsome, but also creeped her out even before she read the title at the bottom which said *The Devil.* That didn't sound good.

Stella pulled the card towards the center of the table. Her frown didn't give her much confidence either.

"What does it mean?"

"It just confirms what you told me. You feel very helpless, and it's understandable given the situation. Please pick another card."

A moment passed before another one caught her eye. This one showed a singular wolf and the word *Strength.* That sounded more promising. She didn't bother to look up at Stella but watched as she placed the card to the left of the first one.

"And another."

How much longer was this going to go on?

She chose and flipped another card. *The Chariot*, this time. It had a picture of two wolves that made her suck in a surprised breath. They looked exactly like her and Dylan's wolf forms.

Stella picked up the card, glancing from the image to her, before placing it back down on the table to the right of the first. "You have an upcoming victory in your future." Zelda could see a small smile on her lips and felt her own mood lift a little. That was the best news she'd heard so far.

"Again."

Zelda repeated the same process and found herself staring at an image of the head Quarter witch sitting in a chair. *Justice*, it said. And it clearly referred to the blood curse she was trying to lift. A shiver ran through her and it took all her strength to suppress the urge to shudder in front of Stella. She didn't need more questions she didn't know if she could answer.

Stella frowned again but didn't comment. "Last card," she said, as she moved it underneath the first card. She tapped her finger above the first. "Place it here, this time."

Zelda flipped the card. An image of a globe lay before her. *The World*, which would normally be as self-explanatory as *Strength* had been. She laid it down on the table as instructed and looked at the collective five images in the cross it made.

Before she could ask what the final card meant, Stella said, "It means success." Without saying more, she gathered all the cards on the table and put them back in the velvet pouch and the box.

Stella then went to a bookshelf and selected a thick tome.

Zelda's heart rate picked up. *That must be it.* It was finally in front of her.

Stella opened the book and Zelda saw it was filled with hand-written notes and diagrams resembling the one Alec had drawn on Dylan's floor. She glanced at Stella from the corner of her eye.

"I'll be right outside if you need me."

The moment the door closed, Zelda quickly flipped through the pages, looking for something the page the Quarter witches wanted.

Once she found it, she read through it, making sure it matched exactly. Satisfied it did, she pulled out her phone, lined up the shot, and took a picture of the page. Checking it was legible, she noticed a completely white image. Frowning, she tried again but got the same result.

She laid her hands on the book and gripped the page. Closing her eyes, she prayed for forgiveness for what she was about to do. Without dwelling on it, she ripped the page out and stuck it in her pocket. She was in the process of closing the book when she noticed the page was back inside. She tried one more time, and quickly closed the book with one hand while patting her pocket with the other. It was still there. She pulled out the page and it had the writing on it, unlike the blank photo.

Now she just had to get out of there.

Her hand touched the handle, quickly pulled it open, and gasped. She was standing back on Bourbon Street. Now there was no doubt that Stella knew what was happening. Or, had at least some vague idea... Regardless of whatever issue existed between the witch and Dylan's father, she was still clearly still their ally. Once everything was over, Zelda would properly thank her.

CHAPTER 19

DYLAN DIDN'T MOVE WHEN HE HEARD FAWN AND Caleb portal onto the lawn. Maybe Stella had told them about the magic ban in the house. He listened to Alec and Ivy greet them and briefly wondered why Edon wasn't also there to immediately get down to business. But maybe that was just him projecting his own impatience.

When he heard them walking up the stairs, he forced himself to stay seated in his spot in the center of the room instead of giving in to the instinct to hide from his childhood friend. He hadn't thought much about how he wanted to reunite with her. He hadn't even decided *when* he was going to bridge the gap he'd caused and let open between them. But he knew without a doubt he wanted to be on equal footing with her and with Zelda at his side, the last part only solidifying once he'd met his Mate.

The door opened and he couldn't stand the pity, sympathy, and sadness he saw in Fawn's expression. Even Caleb looked affected by the sight of him being stuck in wolf form.

She knelt and reaching a hand out as if to pet him but he retreated. He could already picture the hurt he caused without needing to look at her for confirmation. He couldn't handle being comforted by her right now. He didn't care anymore that she was going to have to fix his problem. Edon had been right that this was necessary. But he didn't want her to see him so weak and vulnerable. It was different from when they'd been dating and they'd openly shared feelings and thoughts they had about almost everything.

And he wanted Zelda here. *Where was she?*

It had only been half a day, but her being away only made him feel more vulnerable. And though he tried to suppress his fear of her abandoning him, he was still anxious she'd change her mind again and leave. But he'd never tell his Pack that. Maybe not even Edon.

Fawn stood up and Caleb stepped forward, wrapping his arm around her waist. The sight didn't bother him as much as he expected it to.

She turned to her brother. "Is he stuck like that?"

Alec nodded.

"How long?"

The door opened and Edon stepped in. He answered without a beat. "All day." He held out his hand to her. "I'm Edon. Dylan's Beta."

She accepted the gesture and quickly assessed him. He wondered what she thought of him.

Edon shook Caleb's hand next.

Fawn spoke up, addressing Alec again. "Have you tried anything?"

Alec shook his head. "It happened after I tried to lift a curse placed on him and his Mate. That didn't work and I figured I shouldn't try anything else in case something worse happened."

Fawn's eyes flew to his at the mention of his Mate, but surprisingly, she didn't immediately fixate on the new topic. Without another word, she waved her hand, and a giant book appeared in her hand. He knew instinctively it was her family Grimoire even though he'd never actually seen it. He lay down, waiting for the next thing to happen.

She closed her eyes, touched his closed bedroom door, and mumbled something. "Everyone will think you're sick and no one will come looking for you."

"That's ominous," Edon said. "And you don't know my mother."

"And you don't know my magic. Trust me, no one is going to come barging in or wondering why they haven't seen you around."

He watched Fawn flip through the pages and started prowling, impatient for a game plan.

"Have any ideas?" she asked Caleb.

He expected the centuries-old angel to say yes, but he shook his head. "I never had to deal with witches when I worked for Lucifer."

The last few words came out tightly, and Dylan could see Fawn go uncomfortably still. Clearly, Caleb's history was still a touchy topic. Not that he could blame Fawn for not liking it. Even if it was what had eventually brought them together, no one wanted to think about their soulmate working for the Devil and corrupting souls for evil?

Edon was glancing back and forth between everyone. And had Dylan been able to psychically communicate with him, he would've filled him in. He hated being unable to talk to anyone. Even surrounded by almost all of the most important people in his life, he'd never felt lonelier without a way to communicate with them.

Fawn finally stopped on a page and showed the book to her brother while Caleb looked over her shoulder.

Curious, Dylan raised himself on his hind legs and saw a page with more diagrams than the number Alec had drawn on his floor. Then he read the ingredients needed and recoiled. *Wolfsbane.*

As if hearing his thoughts, Edon said, "No way. That could kill him."

"It's the best chance we have," Fawn replied softly.

"It's *poison.* You can't do that to him. If this goes wrong, the future of two Packs will be thrown into chaos."

"He's my friend, too, Edon. I would never hurt him."

His Beta stared at her for a moment. He didn't answer and looked to him to make the final decision.

There was only one answer but making a life-threatening choice without his Mate having a say felt wrong. But who knew when she'd be back? The longer he was stuck like this, the less time they had until the Council's extended deadline for completing the Ritual.

He looked around the room and saw everyone waiting for him. He met Fawn's gaze and nodded.

ZELDA FOUND HERSELF IN THE WITCH STORE ONCE again, tapping her foot as she waited in line. It was the first time that there'd ever been actual customers in the shop. Then again, it was also right after lunchtime and maybe tourists were exploring the Quarter more at this time of day. She didn't recognize the woman at the cashier station and decided to look around the store more.

A small table was covered in dolls with varying degrees of realism. A few looked like marionettes, some looked like porcelain dolls, while others looked like soft stuffed animals a child might treat as a best friend. But she didn't have to step closer to know they were fetish dolls, and therefore things she never wanted to be associated with her. Even being in the same room made her skin prickle, as if someone were toying with her, maybe even preparing to stick a needle into her. *Did the coven have dolls of her and Dylan?* They might have even had ones of their parents. She shuddered at the thought. She wasn't sure if that was true, but the fear didn't go away.

Another table displayed a multi-colored collection of crystals. On one side, there were jewelry stands for earrings, necklaces, bracelets, and rings. Each was labeled with the significance of the crystal. On the opposite end of the table, there were different colored velvet pouches. A sign in front of them revealed them to be Hoodoo Bones or Voodoo Runes, carved out of different crystals based on the bag instead of real bones like she expected. Then again, who knew how authentic these items were.

If a normal human butchering the spell on one of their ancestors' gravestone brought a curse upon her and Dylan's families, would they give others the opportunity to do the same or worse? It would just be a disaster in the making.

But she could still feel very real magic in the shop. It emanated from the secret back half of the store. A red light above the dividing curtain was lit. A sign next to it indicated it meant there was a fortune-telling session in progress. She'd never noticed that before. And while she trusted Stella Belgrave to give her a tarot card reading, she wasn't certain that the witches wouldn't secretly curse her further while supposedly giving her insight into her future.

"Excuse me? Can I help you?"

Zelda turned her attention back to the woman at the counter. The last of the customers had gone and it was her turn now. Now that she was looking at her, she was mortal. Zelda squinted. Did she know about the reality of witches and magic?

The curtain moved and the witch she normally spoke to stepped forward. "Why don't you join me in my office?"

Zelda took the invitation and quickly followed her.

Once they were in the office, behind the same door she'd gone through to get to New York. "What are you doing here?"

She pulled out the ripped page and held it out. "Here."

A single eyebrow ticked up in surprise. "Already?"

Zelda shrugged.

The woman took the paper. "You still have two more to go."

As if she needed the reminder. But now that the only out-of-town portion of her secret mission was over, she was looking forward to reuniting with Dylan and their Packs.

Merging with the crowd of people moving through Bourbon Street, Zelda started making her way out of town. As she went, she felt eyes on her, the same way she had in the lake with Dylan during the pre-Ritual cleansing. It had slipped her mind with everything else happening, but now the memory came back full force. Of course, it all made sense now. They had known since the beginning that she and Dylan were getting closer and that their curse would be called into effect for the second time. But why they were watching her *now*, after she'd already done what they'd asked of her. At least a part of it. Now she was working on the rest.

She picked up her speed and once the crowd cleared out, and soon found herself far from any human building. Zelda moved further towards the bayous and Shifted. As always, the pain was awful, but she didn't let it consume her mind to the point of distracting her from seeing Dylan again. And for the first time, thinking about something else—thinking about her Mate—actually made the pain more bearable. She took off running.

DYLAN WAS OVER IT. FAWN HAD BEEN TRYING to cast the same spell for the past two hours, with only a brief lunch break. And being forced to eat off a plate on the floor was humiliating. Not that Alec,

Fawn, Ivy, or Caleb were trying making him feel bad about it as they ate in a circle on the floor so they wouldn't leave him out.

The twins had sandwiched him between them while Edon and Annabelle sat across from him.

"I don't understand what I'm doing wrong," Fawn bemoaned while Caleb rubbed her back. "We have the ingredients," she gestured to the desk which was now covered in small bowls with salt, wolfsbane, water, and mandrake leaves. There was also a bowl of burning sage, which supposedly prevented their conversations in the room from being overheard by anyone else. Given his father hadn't burst in, he assumed it was working.

He shuddered. He'd had to take three separate sips of that each time Fawn tried the spell, only to hack up his stomach contents each time. Edon had thought ahead and brought him a bucket.

"I drew the diagrams correctly..." Fawn trailed off. She placed her plate on the ground and retrieved the spellbook. She glanced between her drawings on the floor and the ones made by her ancestors.

Alec held his hand out for the Grimoire. He studied it for a few moments before putting the giant tome back on the desk.

They shared a look and Dylan knew it was now a psychic conversation. They'd always been intuitive even before they knew about magic, but now they had the ability to have an actual conversation the same way werewolves could with each other. He tried to read their expressions, but they were both impossible to read.

He heard a sound at the end of the property and quickly sat up.

A minute later, his bedroom door opened, and his Mate stood in the threshold.

And then he did one of the most embarrassing things ever. He ran up to her like a common dog and covered her in kisses. He wasn't ashamed of being happy to see his Mate, but not being able to be on the same level as her still stung.

Luckily, she very quickly knelt down and hugged him around his neck. His heart rate kicked up, but he also felt an overwhelming peace wash over him. *You're back!*

She pressed her forehead against his. *I missed you, too.*

He breathed a sigh of relief. The witches had taken a lot of things from him, including his future with his Mate, but they hadn't completely silenced him.

He felt her raise her head and then stiffen, and he knew things still weren't perfect in his world.

WHEN ZELDA HAD WALKED IN, SHE'D NOTICED THERE were six people with Dylan instead of the four she'd left, but then all she'd been able to focus on was Dylan. It hadn't been more than a day, but it still felt like it was way too long since she last saw him, and it was the best homecoming she'd ever experienced.

But then curiosity got the better of her and she looked back at the group. Sitting next to Alec was a girl who looked just like him. His sister, Fawn. And she'd been called in once she had been gone. Were they just waiting for her to be gone before they brought in Dylan's ex?

She stood up but couldn't force her to move closer. Edon had to know about her, but he'd never said anything. She wondered what he thought of Fawn. Did he like her more than her? He clearly liked her enough to call her in when Dylan clearly hadn't before.

Fawn got up and walked over to her. She held out her hand. "I'm Fawn. And you are?" Her curious expression seemed genuine, but Zelda remembered that she likely could read her mind. And she'd been telegraphing her insecurities to probably everyone except the other werewolves in the room.

That was mortifying.

She shook Fawn's hand, praying she didn't bring any of her thoughts up. "I'm—"

Before she could finish answering, Edon was standing next to her and said, "Alpha Makris, and Dylan's Mate." Edon was backing her up, and it felt like a turning point in their relationship. Anna seemed to immediately like her, but Dylan's Beta had taken more convincing. She wondered what changed his mind.

The young witch's eyes widened fractionally in surprise, and her hand dropped. Did she not know about her? Or had they just never told her specifics?

The other new addition to the group stood up and placed a hand around Fawn's waist. Clearly, this was her soulmate. "I'm Caleb," he said, offering his hand.

She shook it, and she could tell that he emanated more power than Alec but not Fawn. And it was somehow different. Unlike Ivy, he didn't offer to fill in any of the blanks. He didn't show any surprise like Fawn, but he was clearly conducting his own inspection of her.

"Have you been able to come up with anything?" Zelda asked, already anticipating their answer given her Mate was still a wolf inside the house.

"I tried a bunch of things" Fawn said, surprising her. "But nothing seems to be working."

That didn't surprise her, but she was still disappointed. Two witches were clearly not better than one.

She noticed the food on the ground and walked towards the door. "I'll be right back." She needed food before she could go up against a group of vampires. She'd never done it before, but she assumed she'd need all her strength. She could've easily gone to a restaurant in the Quarter, but she'd missed Dylan so much, that she'd decided to come here before completing the second part of her mission.

To her surprise, Ivy followed her out. Alec and Ivy hadn't said anything to her since she'd returned. Alec didn't seem to care, but the siren was staring at her again, her brow furrowed.

"What?" she asked, pulling out a plate and layering it with leftover meat from the fridge, and a fork from the drawer.

Ivy filled a glass of water for her and passed it over. "You're planning to leave again."

So, she *could* read minds?

"Don't look so alarmed. I'm just really good at reading body language. Anyway, I want to go with you this time."

Zelda took a large bite and chewed. She took a sip of water to wash it down. "Why?"

"Because there's clearly something you need help with. Where are we going?"

"Bold of you to assume I'll let you come along."

Ivy didn't even bother to argue her point, and Zelda sighed. She should've known better.

"Know anything about vampires?" she asked.

Interest lit in the siren's eyes, and she raised a single eyebrow. "Do you often go looking for trouble?"

Zelda shrugged. "It's still daylight."

"Let's go."

Footsteps sounded on the stairs and Alec soon appeared. He was frowning. Zelda wondered if it was his default expression or if she just annoyed him.

Before he could say anything, Ivy spoke up "Girls trip. You're not invited." They shared a heated look that seemed equal parts frustration and attraction. She bet they were having a silent conversation.

Zelda looked away.

Ivy kissed him quickly. "I'll see you later."

He didn't look placated, but he didn't object either. He did pull her in for another kiss, prompting Ivy to let out a tinkling laugh. Hypnotic, even, and it made complete sense that she was a siren.

Ivy broke the kiss and strode toward the back door before he could change his mind. "I'm driving," she declared.

Zelda tossed her the keys on the way out, leaving Alec behind.

CHAPTER 20

DYLAN SAW THE CAR PEEL AWAY WITH Ivy in the driver seat and Zelda riding shotgun.

She hadn't even told him she was leaving.

Fawn stood next to him silently, also watching the scene below.

Alec was sulking in the corner.

"Where are they going?" Fawn asked.

"Vampire den," he answered tightly. "Ivy shut me out before I could figure out why."

He'd overheard their conversation in the kitchen and heard the silence during Alec and Ivy's conversation, but he hadn't even been able to hear Zelda's thoughts.

It was already bad enough they were fighting the Quarter witches. Why would she be going to the natural enemies of werewolves? What if she got hurt? And he couldn't go help her.

"Fawn, can you go help them?"

Everyone turned to Caleb, who had barely said anything since he and Fawn had arrived days ago. Marcus had finally seen them and given all four of them the last guest room, what had briefly been Zelda's room, without any comment.

Dylan bet Alec and Fawn weren't happy about having to share a room again. He snickered and his friend shot him a dirty look as if he knew what he was thinking.

"Don't you need me here?" Fawn asked her brother.

He shook his head. "I think we're just stuck."

Dylan lay down. He knew it was true, but hearing it confirmed still hit him with the weight of an anvil.

Caleb continued. "They'll feel better if you're with Ivy and Zelda."

"What about you? You won't be worried about me?"

"The three of you together will be a force to be reckoned with. And you have magic when they don't. I'm not worried, but please be careful." He hugged her to his side and kissed her forehead.

Dylan had expected to feel some jealousy when they arrived, but it hadn't bothered him at all other than make him sad he couldn't do the same with Zelda.

When Caleb let Fawn go, she shared a look with her brother and quickly disappeared through a portal.

He still had no real idea of what was going on, but if Ivy and Fawn had Zelda's back, he knew that she'd be okay. She just had to be.

T HE CAR SKIDDED TO A STOP PARALLEL TO the street, and Zelda finally let go of the dashboard in front of her. "I am *never* letting you drive again. Were you trying to kill us?"

The siren scoffed. "I was trying to get us here quickly. I assume you're on a short timeline, so you should be *thanking* me."

She didn't answer and instead got out of the car, slamming the car door. It wasn't loud enough to wake the dead. Vampires slept during the day, right? She leaned against the side while waiting for her companion to join her.

Ivy got out and locked the door, coming around to her side.

"So, vampires, huh?" It was maybe the hundredth time she had heard the question in the past twenty minutes.

"Yep..." Zelda hadn't given her any real answers, not wanting to further test how much she could say while under the Quarter witch's spell ensuring the secrecy of her mission.

Ivy stared straight ahead at the large building in front of them. "I assume you have a plan beyond just walking into the den. You do know there will be at least ten vampires, right?"

"How do you know so much about vampires?"

The woman blushed. "I've had some experience with them." But then she got indignant. "The last time I ran into these vampires, though, the head vampire was a sexist ass and I *may* have picked a fight with him."

"Then why are you coming back?" And won't him seeing her put him on the attack? How was that supposed to *help* the situation?

"Are you both seriously going in without a plan to get out?"

Zelda turned and saw Fawn leaning on the door of the car. Or, where the car had been.

What had she done?

"We won't need it," Fawn said. "But you do have to tell us what we're doing here."

"How did you find us?"

"I'm a witch. Do you know how simple a locator spell is in the grand scheme of magic? Now, answer my question."

"It wasn't a question."

She raised an eyebrow, and Zelda relented.

"I need something from them..." How far could she go? "Blood."

Fawn's eyes narrowed ever so slightly, and Zelda could practically see the wheels turning in her head.

"I'm assuming from the oldest," the witch correctly guessed.

Ivy shot her friend a surprised look, and it made Zelda feel better to know she wasn't the only one confused by Fawn's knowledge.

"I can get us in, and I can get us home, but if they start attacking, I can't hold them all off at once. I'm out of practice."

When had the witch been able to defend against that many assailants at once? And why would she need to?

Ivy shrugged. "I'm fine."

Zelda took in the petite frame of the siren. She couldn't picture her being able to throw down against vampires with super strength and super speed, but she also knew to never underestimate a fighter based on size. It was less about what you had to work with and more about *how* you worked with it. She just hoped Ivy actually knew what she was doing and wasn't simply talking a big game.

"If you need blood, how are you going to get it?" Ivy asked. "We can't exactly stick a needle in him and wait for a vial to fill up. They'd probably drain us before that even happened."

Fawn pulled a hairpin out of her bun and held it in her hands while she muttered what Zelda assumed was a spell. She held the piece of metal out, saying, "If you can prick him with this, I can then multiply the drop of blood into however much we need."

"Let's go." Zelda grabbed the handle and pulled the door open. It was time to get this over with.

Walking inside, all she could see was darkness for a second as her eyes adjusted. And then she saw them. If she didn't know where she was, she'd assume the people splayed out all over the furniture were college students who had gotten wasted and were still hungover as hell. But these were vampires sleeping the day away. She just hoped they'd stay that way a bit longer.

The moment she thought it, their eyes started opening, red and silver irises glowing in the dark. She should've known better than to ask for the impossible. Once they were safe, she'd ask Ivy why there were different colors, but now wasn't the time.

She dodged left as one went for her neck, all the while searching for who was the oldest vampire. She probably should've asked Ivy to describe him before they barged in, given she'd already met him.

She heard another vampire approaching but didn't move fast enough. It grabbed her from behind, and she quickly drove an elbow behind her, knocking them off her before any teeth could pierce her neck. It hissed at her and she quickly kicked its kneecap in.

They kept coming, even with others fighting Ivy and Fawn separately. Soon, six were all over her, and she felt panic rising as they began to outnumber her. Going on autopilot, she dodged and weaved as best as she could, suffering some scrapes from sharp fingernails in the process. A few times, some teeth got too close for comfort.

Before any of them could bite her, they all retreated, leaving her and her friends alone. Ivy looked as confused as she felt.

"It's not polite to eat our guests before first having a conversation," a silky voice said. "I thought I taught you all better manners."

Out of the shadows came a man who somehow stood out from the others despite sharing the same pale skin and sharp teeth as all the others. *This* was clearly the oldest vampire, the one she'd been looking for.

He scanned the room, taking in Fawn, Ivy, and her. He plastered on a plastic smile, like a predator playing with its prey knowing full well he was already the victor. She hoped that wasn't the case. "Breaking and entering is a crime, ladies, and not at all becoming of the fairer sex." He stepped up to Ivy. "I believe I told you last time you were not welcome here."

The siren shrugged. "I don't do well with authority. Especially male authority. So, bite me."

He stared at her for a minute, then made a disapproving sound. "Unlike some of my kind, I don't like seafood," he sneered.

Ivy blushed.

Wait, what? Did that mean Ivy had let a vampire bite her before? She was *definitely* asking her about that later.

His gaze shifted again, this time to Fawn. "What have we done to bring down the wrath of a Belgrave witch? We have never offended your family, nor committed any violence against your kind."

"I'm here as a favor to a friend. I'm not here to start a war."

"A smarter werewolf would steer clear of my den. It would be a shame for a face as beautiful as yours to hide an empty head."

"I thought you liked your women that way, Count," Ivy shot back despite Fawn motioning her to stay silent.

Was this Dracula? He looked a lot more... normal... than she expected. Though, a vampire who couldn't blend into humanity probably didn't last very long—despite being immortal.

The vampire in question lifted an eyebrow at her and shook his head, answering her silent question. "I'm old-fashioned, not sexist," he turned and pinned the siren with a pointed look, "as you've been telling your friends."

Of course, he'd been eavesdropping on their conversation outside. But if he'd been awake the whole time, why did he let his minions attack them in the first place?

"You still haven't told me why you're here."

"Don't you already know?" Zelda asked.

"Ah, not so dull, after all. Yes, I do. I was curious as to what lie you'd tell. I was not expecting honesty given your entrance into my home."

"Will you help me?"

"I don't make a habit of giving my essence out to anyone who asks for it."

She glanced back at the darkness, where the twenty vampires had disappeared, then back at him.

"I chose them," he clarified. "They did not come begging and I decided to give charity." He looked her up and down, his eyes assessing her. Despite herself, she wondered what he thought of her. "But if you wanted to become one of my own, you wouldn't have risked getting a deadly vampire bite." He took a step closer. "So, why *do* you want my blood, little wolf, if not for the most obvious reason?"

"We're not going to place a hex on you, if that's what you're worried about," Fawn interjected. "If you give us some of your blood, I'll return the favor if you need something in the future."

Ivy stared hard at her friend, and Zelda found herself wondering yet again what was happening.

The vampire either didn't know or didn't care, because he quickly accepted the offer. "You have a vial, I presume?"

Fawn waved her hand and produced one, then handed it to him. Zelda watched with equal parts disgust and fascination as he bit his finger until it started dripping blood into the small glass container. When it was half-full, no more than a quarter of a teaspoon, his skin healed, and he closed the cap. Instead of handing it over, he took yet another step closer to her.

"I've given you some of my blood. I think it's only fair I ask for a little in return."

"Didn't you say your bite would kill me?"

"I said you wouldn't risk receiving a deadly bite."

Her spine stiffened. "Why?"

He smirked. "It's been a while. It'll be a pleasurable experience. Your friend can attest to that."

Zelda resisted the urge to glance at Ivy and kept her gaze squarely on the vampire in front of her. "Is this another part of the deal?"

He nodded.

This time, she did look away from him, not to see Ivy, but what Fawn thought of the whole affair.

The witch had her eyes trained on him for a moment before her gaze shifted to meet hers. She gave a small, barely perceptible nod.

Zelda tipped her head to the side, baring her neck to the man who was helping her save her Mate.

His hand wrapped around the back of her neck, the other around her waist, holding her still as his teeth pricked her neck.

A gasp of surprise escaped her. She hadn't been expecting the flash of warmth to engulf her body. She swayed on her feet and felt his hand at her back press her tighter against him.

Moments passed and then she started feeling lightheaded. Was he killing her?

She heard someone clear their throat and suddenly she was released. Her head was still spinning when he held out the vial to her. She took it.

"You might want to take a sip to heal faster," he murmured.

"Are you okay?" Ivy asked.

She turned to see the siren standing next to her and felt a wave of dizziness hit her.

The vampire addressed Ivy, "This is the last time I will see you in my home. Two times you've come here, and I've let you go, but do not try for a third."

He hadn't bared his teeth, but that was the most intimidating thing he'd said this whole time.

"Thank you," Zelda managed, her equilibrium returning.

He nodded and turned away, finally disappearing into the dark where the rest of his coven awaited him.

She hoped she never saw another vampire again.

"Where to next?" Fawn asked.

"Home. For now."

The witch waved her hand, opening another portal. "After you."

A N HOUR PASSED BEFORE THEY RETURNED. AND IN that time, Annabelle and Edon had dropped in multiple times to try to distract him and Alec from the fact their soulmates were off fighting vampires. Caleb seemed perfectly fine with the situation, but he didn't know him well enough to spot any tells that might tell him different.

When he'd seen his car magically return, he'd briefly hoped they were back.

"There's no way she keeps her mouth shut around that vampire. What if she gets them killed?" Alec was wondering aloud.

"They're not going to *die*," Caleb growled, clearly frustrated with his brother-in-law's anxiety-fueled ramblings. Maybe he was more affected than he originally let on. "First of all, they're all extremely capable women, and second, we'd feel if something was wro—" His words died off as his brow furrowed. He was sensing something.

"They're outnumbered," Alec groaned.

It appeared he was the only one without a true connection to his Mate. It had to be the curse cutting him off from those around him in yet another way.

"They're fighting," the angel replied. "They've done it before."

"We were all there with them last time."

And it hadn't been pretty back then, either. He had faith in them, but he couldn't control his anxiety much better than Alec was his.

"If you don't stop pacing, I'm going to tie you up."

The door opened, and Edon stood in the threshold. "Should I come back then?"

Dylan let out a laugh, and everyone looked at him again, as if they forgot he was there. If he weren't so preoccupied with the safety of his Mate and his friends, he would've been offended.

"No need," Caleb grunted.

"Well, my mom wants to know if she can get you anything."

"We just had lunch a few hours ago," Alec said.

That never mattered to Esme. She offered food to people when they were already eating. If she could find someone who would eat all day long, she'd provide enough for anyone to do so.

Edon smirked. "Is that a no, then?"

Before Alec could retort, a breeze rushed through the room, and Zelda stumbled through the portal followed by Fawn and Ivy.

The smell of blood—her blood—filled the air, and he immediately jumped to his feet.

Zelda glanced around the room, her gaze landing on him.

"I'm never doing that again," his Mate muttered, turning her head to address Ivy as the girls sat her down on the bed.

And that's when he saw the blood on her neck.

The growl escaped him without a second thought.

Edon quickly echoed it, and Alec stepped closer.

Caleb didn't move, but he was also watching the girls, a frown marring his normally placid expression.

"Had you asked *me*, I would've said not to do it," Ivy huffed, handing her a tissue.

His Mate took it and wiped at the blood, revealing two holes in her neck. " *You're* the one who's done it before. Besides, Fawn said it was a good idea."

Understanding dawned on Caleb's face, and he walked over to Fawn. "Was this smart?"

"It was necessary," Fawn replied.

How was a vampire biting his Mate *necessary*?

"No offense to Fawn, but what does she know about it?" Ivy shot back. "You just said I'm the one with experience in this area."

" *What?*" Alec shouted.

Ivy shot him a look, but it didn't silence him.

"When did you let a vampire bite you?"

"Before we were together. Not that it's any of your business."

"You're my soulmate! Of course, it's my business."

"We both know we had other partners before we finally got together. It's not a big deal."

"Not a—"

Dylan closed his eyes, trying to block out their squabbling. *Are you okay?* he asked Zelda.

She only smiled at him. He wasn't comforted. Why didn't she psychically reply like normal? Was she dying from vampire venom?

He walked over to her and lay his head on her lap.

She rested a hand on his head. "I'm fine," she said. "I'm just still lightheaded. I'll be fine."

"It'll pass soon, Dylan," Fawn added. "But she needs to rest first."

Caleb left first, quickly followed by her. Ivy and Alec walked out together, their heads close and no doubt having an ongoing silent conversation about vampires.

Zelda lay back, her head falling back onto the pillow.

Are you back to stay?

She shook her head, her eyes closing. *I have one more thing I need to do.*

He listened until he heard her breathing slow and stabilize. He crawled closer, lying next to her.

She kept coming back, but when would it be time for her to permanently *stay*?

CHAPTER 21

SOMEONE WAS KNOCKING ON THE DOOR. ZELDA TURNED over and came up against something warm, large, and furry. Opening her eyes, she saw that while she was sleeping, Dylan had moved even closer.

Slowly extricating herself, she gently nudged him.

He blinked blearily at her, his normally brilliant emerald eyes a clouded and muted forest green as he woke up.

Zelda opened the door and found Caleb standing there.

"Can we talk in private?"

She took a surprised step back. She still knew next to nothing about him. And what could he possibly want to talk to her about? She heard Dylan move and was unsurprised when he nudged her aside to guard her legs against the visitor.

Caleb examined her. It seemed everyone in Dylan's life was always sizing her up. His father, his ex-girlfriends, his family friend Stella, and now his ex-girlfriend's soulmate.

Zelda stepped around Dylan and followed Caleb down the stairs and into the empty study. He closed the door and gestured for her to sit in the leather chair.

Instead, she leaned against the desk while he stayed near the entrance. Was he guarding her? Trapping her?

"No," he said. "I'm not trapping you in here. But I want to warn you about the Quarter witches."

"A little late for that."

He ignored her. "They always have a trick. Even if you think things are going perfectly now, know that something will still go wrong."

"And you've dealt with this coven before?"

He nodded. "But Fawn doesn't know."

What did that have to do with anything?

"Zelda, I'm an angel. I've been around for a *long* time, and I've never seen a deal with a coven go well. From the Quarter witches, the ones in Salem, or those in European royal courts. Inter-species deals are never fair."

"The one I made with the vampire was."

His eyes drifted to her neck. "I wouldn't be so sure."

"What does that mean?"

He met her gaze. "By letting him feed on you, you gave him immunity to a werewolf bite."

"Oh."

"See what I mean? I just think you should be very careful. You've already completed two tasks out of the three."

"How—"

"Stella told me."

"Does Fawn know?"

He shook his head.

"Why not?"

"She didn't want to color her daughter's judgment of you."

"I'm guessing she doesn't like me."

"Fawn is very protective of the people she loves. And she doesn't trust easily." He paused. "I didn't exactly help with that last part." He said it lightly, but Zelda knew he was sharing something important.

"I think we're similar."

Before she could ask how, he continued.

"We'll do anything for our soulmate, especially to prove ourselves after making an early mistake."

She was speechless. Did he know all of it? She hadn't gotten the sense that Caleb and Dylan were friends, but maybe she'd been wrong. Or maybe Alec had told him everything? But that didn't make much sense. Dylan's best friend wouldn't betray his trust—even if it was to family.

"I don't know the particulars. No one has told me, and I don't read people's minds. You just publicly project your thoughts."

Alec had said something similar.

"It's not a big deal. I know other wolves can't hear your thoughts unless you mean them to, so you'd have no reason to believe anyone could read them. Anyway, my point is, I didn't need someone to tell me we're similar. I could see it. I'm very good at reading people, and in this case, it takes one to know one."

"It worked out for you."

He nodded. "Because I quickly learned not to fix it alone."

"The girls came with me last time."

"We both know Ivy didn't give you much of a choice and that Fawn surprised both of you. This time, you might want to ask for help. I'm sure you'll find it."

"Why are you telling me any of this?"

"Because you mean the world to Dylan, and Fawn cares about him. And I try to do everything I can to make her happy."

When she didn't answer, he added, "Just think about what I said."

He reached for the door.

"Will you come with me tonight?"

"I recommend Fawn also accompany us."

She'd be third-wheeling on what was supposed to be a private mission, but if Caleb was right about the Quarter witches, having back up of any kind was worth it. And this was a freaking *angel* and a witch who she trusted had her back—even if only because of her relationship with Dylan. She nodded.

"We can leave when you're ready."

He opened the door and Fawn stood there, an expectant expression on her face.

"You're not leaving without me, I hope."

He dropped a kiss on her forehead. "Never," Caleb answered.

Zelda went back up to the bedroom. Dylan was waiting by the door, his tail slightly wagging.

I have to go now, but I'll be back soon.

A large paw landed on her, holding her in place. His large sad eyes met hers. *Be safe.*

She nodded and kissed his snout. *I'll be back in no time.*

He released her, and she left without another word. The next time she saw him, he'd be human again.

Downstairs, Fawn and Caleb waited for her. They were holding hands and reached out for hers. She completed the circle, hoping none of the werewolves would see them and ask what was happening.

"Where are we going?" Fawn asked.

"St. Louis Cathedral."

Unlike when Stella had enchanted a doorway, and Fawn had created a portal, this time, she felt her stomach knot and her chest tighten as the wind whipped around her. She closed her eyes, and when she opened them again, she was standing outside the darkened church.

"Do you know what we're getting?"

"I can picture it, but I can't describe it."

Without warning, Fawn placed her hands on Zelda's forehead. A burning sensation ripped its way through her mind, and Zelda couldn't contain the scream that escaped.

"*Fawn*," Caleb said. "We talked about this."

"Sorry," she said to me sheepishly.

"What did you just do?"

"I lowered the barriers in your mind. You had a really big wall up."

"I thought you told me I project my thoughts," I said, addressing the angel.

"You do." He didn't elaborate.

"It was the Quarter witch, right?"

"Yes. Anyway, we're looking for a wooden statue. She called it an idol. It's hidden somewhere in the church."

"Let's go."

Fawn reached for the door, then hissed out a breath.

"What's the matter?"

"I can't get in. It's warded against witches. Probably why they needed you to get this back for them." She sighed. "I guess I'll stay out here. I can cloak the church so no one will see us or think anything is suspicious. Caleb, go help her."

"I don't want to leave you."

"You were all for me going alone on the vampire mission."

"You weren't alone there. You had Zelda and Ivy."

"Caleb, we don't have time for this. We need to get this done so the witches can fix Dylan, and then he and Zelda can finally live happily ever after."

Zelda reached for the door and it opened easily. The hair on the back of her neck lifted. Someone had left it unlocked.

Caleb kissed Fawn then followed her inside.

He closed the door and closed his eyes.

"What are you doing?" she whispered.

"Mapping the place. Give me a moment."

She waited. He looked like he was meditating.

His eyes opened and he moved so quickly, he became a blur in her vision, even with her enhanced werewolf senses. He stood at the pulpit, white wings outstretched on either side, making him look like a fierce opponent. If any of the humans of the congregation saw him, they'd probably faint. When he'd said he was an angel, she hadn't even thought about him having wings.

"It's somewhere over here," he said. He jerked his shoulders forward and the wings snapped in, disappearing from view.

She blinked, still in some shock at seeing them.

She walked quickly up the aisle to meet him, coming to stand behind the pulpit and stared up at the Greco-Roman marble display. In the center was a painting of light raining down from a golden cross in the heavens, complete with angel statues. Though beautiful, it made her shudder. Something about this church felt off.

Looking closer, she saw what looked like a golden sun. The center was a sky blue but seemed so blank in comparison to the ornate design all around it. And it looked like there was a singular point of dirt on it, too small for a human eye to detect.

Without thinking, she touched it, only to feel a raised surface. A button. She pressed it and felt the floor rumble.

"What did you do?" Caleb asked.

She didn't see anything happen. "I don't know."

One of the gold-trimmed rectangular panels on the base of columns moved, revealing a hidden compartment. Inside stood the statue they were looking for.

"Is that it?"

She nodded and tentatively reached for it, half-expecting an Indiana Jones-level booby trap to spring, but nothing happened. She grabbed it, and the panel immediately closed.

"Let's get out of here," she muttered.

The moment they stepped outside, she tensed. Standing in front of her was Raoul in wolf form.

He lunged, but she was jerked back, and her vision suddenly blocked by a wall of white.

She turned around and saw Caleb, encircling her with his wings.

"What about Fawn?"

"She's busy." He turned his head and she followed his gaze. His soulmate was standing off to the side, her hands raised, and clearly chanting something under her breath. And that's when she noticed the air shimmering in an ethereal curtain, on the other side of which stood all the werewolves who had deserted her to follow her former Beta.

"I don't see your *Mate* here. Did you leave him already? Or did he dump you?"

"What are you doing here?"

"I came to get that."

She gripped the idol tighter. "Why?"

"Because the witches made me a deal, too." He began circling, but Caleb did the same.

If she Shifted, would she injure the angel?

No, he answered inside her head. *You'd be vulnerable if you did.*

But I can't fight him well now.

Caleb slipped the statue from her hand, concealing it behind his wings. *Do it now.*

She did, and it was the fastest she'd ever done so. She saw Fawn send her a quick wink before returning to maintaining the shield.

Caleb stepped away and now there was no barrier between her and her former best friend. The man who had become her enemy in such a short amount of time.

To her surprise, he didn't lunge again. His assessing eyes were searching for the idol, and she hoped that Caleb had some way to keep it from him.

What deal? she demanded.

To set things right.

She had a feeling they meant very different things.

You were meant to be my Mate.

The witches clearly hadn't told him about the curse guaranteeing her union to Dylan, but why would they do that? If they wanted to tear them apart, why do it now when they had so many earlier opportunities?

He broke up our Pack, and he's not even by your side. Pathetic.

Because he can't leave his home—*their* home. But she wasn't about to tell him that. He might send his Pack to ambush the Morsure Pack, and who knew if Alec would be as effective as his sister in protecting everyone.

You were supposed to leave New Orleans.

I would never leave you behind. Now, give it to me. I don't want to hurt you.

That didn't stop you before.

The thought was out before she could catch it, and that set him off.

He lunged again, knocking her and pinning her to the ground. He went for her neck, the same tender spot where the vampire had fed hours earlier. She kicked him, knocking him off balance, and making him miss his target, but he still stayed on top of her.

Caleb knocked him off, and she watched Raoul swipe at the angel's wings, tearing feathers out with his claws. She saw Caleb wince and searched for an opening.

He saw what she was doing and moved out of the way, giving her a clear shot.

She pounced, her jaw clamping around Raoul's throat, something she hadn't been able to do during their last fight. It wasn't like the play sparring they'd done growing up, and she had every intention to kill him if need be, but she still remembered her friend and pleaded.

Don't make me do this.

You wouldn't.

Closing her eyes, she bit him.

He went limp beneath her, and only when she was sure he couldn't attack her again, did she release him.

I'm sorry, she said.

He was dying, forcing the defectors back to her Pack, and their thoughts flooded into her mind. Most with pure shock, and some with newfound, if not begrudging, respect for her.

She glanced over and nodded at Fawn, who lowered her hands and the veil now that the larger threat had passed. They wouldn't attack her now that she was their Alpha again.

Movement out of the corner of her eye caught her attention. Caleb stood with the head Quarter witch by his side, his hand gripping her upper arm. She hadn't even seen him leave.

"Lift the curse," he said, handing her the idol.

"I need my coven," she answered.

Fawn stepped up to her. "You can channel me." She held out both hands. "But don't try to take my magic. You can't."

The woman didn't argue. She took Fawn's hands and began chanting. A second passed before Fawn joined her as if knowing the words by heart. Maybe she did, although it didn't sound like what Alec had tried back at the house.

They kept going until the witch finally let go of Fawn. "It is done."

"How do I know?" Zelda asked. "You went behind my back and made another deal."

"You can see for yourself." She waved her hand and Dylan stood before her in human form.

She ran to him, hugging him close and showering him with tiny kisses all over his face.

Then she took a step back and glanced at Fawn. "Is this real?"

She took Dylan's hand in hers and closed her eyes. She looked back at Zelda. "He's real."

"And you lifted the blood curse on both our families?"

The older witch nodded. "I swear on my ancestors' souls. May I go now?"

Again, she looked to Fawn, who nodded. "It was part of the incantation."

"Yes. And thank you."

The woman nodded and disappeared in a puff of smoke, not unlike that of the Wicked Witch of the West in *The Wizard of Oz*.

Dylan suddenly moved, and Zelda followed him to Raoul's prone body. What he said next surprised her more than anything that had happened that day.

"Do you want me to save him?"

H E WATCHED HER FACE AS SHE STARED DOWN at the man who'd been her Beta before he had attacked both of them and waited for her answer. He didn't know which he wanted more. But whatever she said, he'd do. She'd saved him, and she was his Mate. The only thing after this was to redo the Ritual, and all would be right in the world. And if Zelda required Raoul to be alive in that perfect world, he'd do it.

Finally, she nodded. "But it's up to him. Raoul, can you hear me? Dylan's here. He can save you."

He opened his eyes slowly, settling on him.

"If you agree to join my Pack, my bite will heal you," Dylan added.

"Please say yes," she said.

He turned his gaze towards Zelda. "I'd rather die than live a lifetime seeing you with him."

Seeing his Mate's stricken expression made him growl. "You'll get your wish." He stood up and pulled Zelda with him. "Let's go home."

She nodded, still staring at Raoul.

Fawn came over, as did Caleb. They formed a circle and held hands.

"Brace yourselves," Fawn said.

When he'd been unceremoniously transported to Zelda in human form, he was unprepared. This time, he knew what to expect. For the second time in a few minutes, his insides felt like they were being turned inside out, and then they were back home.

"We need to tell the Council we can do the Ritual again," he said.

Zelda nodded but stayed silent.

Fawn and Caleb slipped away, walking back to their room upstairs. They, along with Alec and Ivy, had been staying in the guest room that had briefly been Zelda's. He bet the twins didn't like sharing space again, especially with their soulmates present.

He placed a hand at Zelda's back and guided her into the kitchen. He poured a glass of water for each of them and sat her down at the counter. He took the spot next to her and pulled her in close.

She lay her head on his shoulder and let out a shuddering breath.

He just rubbed circles on her back. He wasn't going to push her to talk about it until she was ready.

When moments passed and she didn't move, he brought her glass to her lips. "Please drink some."

She did silently, not making a move to hold the glass herself. He put it back down and kissed her temple.

He saw someone enter and made eye contact with Bailey. She opened her mouth to speak, but he growled. For the first time ever, she immediately shut her mouth and walked away without getting what she wanted. But he heard her saying, "He's back, everyone."

"Let's go upstairs," he said.

Zelda didn't move, so he lifted her into his arms, leaving the water downstairs. *Edon, I left two glasses on the counter. Can you bring them to my room? Knock first.*

You got it.

He walked up the stairs to his room, nudged the door open, and settled his Mate onto the bed. She quickly curled up on her side. He lay down beside her and positioned her head on his chest, over his beating heart.

"I thought he'd say yes," she finally said. "I don't get why he didn't."

He'd been very clear during his refusal, but he wasn't about to point that out. But even then, it didn't totally make sense to him either. He and Zelda had been such close friends for so long. To die while so diametrically opposed only added insult to injury.

"I'm sorry," he said.

"Me, too."

He hated to switch topics, but they had big things that still needed their attention. "We have two days before our deadline," he started. "We can wait until the last day if you want."

She shook her head. "No. We've waited long enough."

"Are you sure? You're grieving right now. It's okay if you want to."

She sat up, and he followed suit.

When she leaned in and kissed him, he let her take the lead, unsure of her intentions.

It was a gentle, drawn-out kiss. And when she pulled away, she rested her forehead against his. "I'm sure."

He smiled in return. "Well, okay then."

ZELDA DIDN'T REMEMBER FALLING ASLEEP. WHEN SHE WOKE up, Dylan was by her side and in human form. She smiled and kissed him, but her happy relief was tempered by the memory of Raoul's final words to her.

A tear slipped out, and there was Dylan's hand, wiping it away.

"I'm sorry," she said.

"It's okay." He kissed her cheek. "I'll bring up breakfast, okay?"

She swung her legs out of the bed. "I don't want to mope."

"Okay." He climbed out of bed and she saw that he'd changed into pajamas at some point.

She looked down and saw the same. Had he dressed her?

"Hope you don't mind," he said. "I didn't think you'd want to sleep all night in jeans."

She walked up to him and kissed him. "Thank you."

They got ready for the day and walked downstairs.

Marcus was waiting for them by the staircase.

"It's good to see you again, son. You, too, Zelda."

"Thank you," she answered.

What had changed his mind?

Esme rushed up to Dylan and pulled him in for a hug. "I'm so glad you're feeling better. Edon wouldn't let me come in to check on you."

When would that have stopped her?

It was her turn next and Zelda found herself in a tight embrace. "I'm so glad you're both okay. I barely saw you, either. And Edon wouldn't say *anything* about it. I was so worried about you."

Edon came over and gave her a side hug. "Glad to have you back."

Annabelle gave her a quick hug. "I'm so glad it's all over."

She saw Bailey standing in the corner watching the small celebration. A moment passed and she left without saying a word, nasty or nice. Zelda supposed she was getting better.

Do you want me to tell my father to reconvene the Council?

Yes.

"Dad, can Zelda and I talk to you privately?"

"Of course." He led the way to the study.

"We're ready to redo the Ritual," her Mate said.

Marcus leaned forward on the desk. "Son, your Mate went through hell last time. You were just really sick. And now you know about the blood curse. Why on Earth would you go through that again?"

"Because we lifted the curse."

Clearly, Dylan was leaving out the extra curse they'd just dealt with. It was moot anyway, so she wouldn't bring it up either.

"How—"

"I made a deal with the Quarter witches," Zelda answered.

He frowned.

"They lifted the curse in exchange for me helping them undo the damage you and my father caused. Fawn verified it was real. We can finally be together like we're supposed to be."

Marcus' gaze jumped between her and his son as they spoke. Finally, he said, "Thank you, Zelda. I'm happy to have such a good daughter-in-law."

"We're not getting married, Dad."

He shrugged and stood up. "I'll gather the Council. We can do it tonight if you're both ready." He took a breath. "I'm sorry if I was supportive before, but I'm very happy you found each other."

"Thank you, Alpha Stone."

"Marcus," he corrected. "We'll be family soon."

She smiled. "Marcus."

EPILOGUE

DYLAN ZIPPED UP THE BACK OF ZELDA'S DRESS. It was the same white won she'd worn last week when they tried the Ritual.

He'd suggested borrowing a white dress from one of the other she-wolves in their Packs, but she'd refused.

"It wasn't the dresses fault. And you paid good money for this."

With everything that had been going on, he hadn't even bothered to look at the digital receipts of her shopping spree with Annabelle and the sisters.

He'd decided to pick a different white shirt, but for all intents and purposes, he was also wearing the same outfit. It didn't really matter since they'd be Shifting out of them soon enough.

"Ready?" he asked.

She kissed him lightly on the lips and smoothed her hands down the front of his chest. "Yes."

He held the doors open for her on their way down to the lake.

The Council was waiting for them in robes. So was his father, fulfilling his role of Alpha to preside over all Rituals in his Pack. But he wished Edon and his friends were allowed to be there. He wondered if Zelda wished any of her wolves were there as support, even though she'd also grown closer to Annabelle, Ivy, and Fawn.

"Alpha Makris, Dylan Stone," announced Elder Kai, "you may Shift and the Ritual will begin."

They did, and Zelda surprised him by laying down first. He didn't care either way, but her following tradition after everything they'd gone through only showed him just how committed she was to their Mate bond.

Carefully, he stood over her and opened his jaws around the base of her throat, the same side where the vampire bit her. He wanted to erase all signs of the other Supernatural on her When he felt her teeth tickled his neck and it activated the primal urge to successfully Mark his Mate. He bit a millisecond before she did, and he tasted her coppery blood for a few seconds, feeling the mental division between them fall like an overflowing dam. He let go and she did the same.

I'm here, Zelda, he said, merely thinking it instead of projecting it.

She licked the spot where she'd bit him. *I never thought I'd be so happy to have you in my head.*

He licked her neck, too. Then her snout, earning him a rush of elation on her end.

Polite applause pulled him out of the moment, and he let Zelda up so they could both face the Council again.

"The Ritual is complete. Congratulations, both of you," Elder Raghnall said. "And now, we feast."

Without a formal agreement, he and Zelda raced back to the house, then Shifted at the kitchen door. He lifted her into his arms and walked her over the threshold, and they were met with both Packs and his friends. They all burst into applause, and he felt his own pride and Zelda's embarrassment-tinged happiness. It should've been confusing to experience her emotions in addition to his own, but it felt absolutely perfect.

They walked through the crowd to the large table reserved for them and those who were witnesses to the Ritual. Esme served them each a plate before sitting back down at her table with their closest friends.

Everyone sat down with their food and waited for Marcus to give the signal to start eating.

I did a little remodeling, Fawn's voice sounded in his mind. *Your entire Pack will fit inside comfortably, and the guest house will be available. Maybe I'll even get to see it if you ever extend an invite.*

Thank you for everything you've done.

She nodded.

Dylan turned his attention back to his father when Marcus stood. "Now that my son has found his Mate and is forever bonded to her, I hereby renounce my title as Alpha. Effective immediately. Congratulations to our new Alpha and Luna. Dig in, everyone."

Dylan stared at his father. He hadn't been expecting that at all.

Zelda's hand found his under the table, interlacing their fingers.

He looked to her and she smiled. "Congratulations, *Alpha*."

"You, too, Luna." He kissed her, ignoring the wolf whistle Alec and Edon let out in unison. *I know you didn't want to give up your Alpha title. Are you okay with this? I'll happily call you Alpha. It's our Pack.*

You can make it up to me by letting me be Alpha in private.

He grinned. *Deal.*

ZELDA LAUGHED AS DYLAN DROPPED HER ON THE bed. She scrambled back towards the headboard as he crawled towards her. "Are you *sure* this is okay? We're in charge of the Pack now." They'd each barely eaten half the food on their plates, too amped up to stay downstairs any longer, but she still felt weird about leaving everyone so publicly.

"Exactly," he said, punctuating it with a kiss. "We're in charge, which means we can delegate to our awesome Beta while we get some privacy." He kissed her again. "Besides, everyone who might tell us no has been through this before. They know how *excited* newly-Mated couples get."

"In that case," she undid the button at his collar. "Take this off."

"Yes, Alpha."

She watched his fingers fly. "You know I was joking about that."

"But I wasn't." He tossed his shirt to the ground. "What next?"

"For starters, you can help me get out of this dress." When she'd put it on, it felt light enough for the Louisiana summer, but now she felt like she was burning up. Though that was more Dylan's fault that the weather.

"With pleasure. Turn around."

She sat up and gave her back to him.

He pulled down one strap and kissed her newly-bared skin and worked his way up her neck. Each press of his lips made her skin get hotter with need. Then he did the same thing on the other side.

She was so caught up in what he was doing with his mouth that she forgot what she'd even asked for by the time he started unzipping her. And then he traced her spine with a finger followed by his mouth.

"Dylan..."

His only answer was a light hum against her skin.

She spun around, kicking off the dress and pushing it to the floor. "You're driving me crazy."

"Sorry."

She climbed onto his lap and kissed him and bit his lip a little harder than normal. "No, you're not." She pushed on his chest until he lay down, his head practically hanging off the foot of the bed. "I think you enjoy it."

"You have to admit you like it."

She pulled back. "I do *not.*"

"You don't have to say it. I can feel everything you are now."

As if she could forget. His carnal hunger was like putting her own on steroids. If things didn't move to the next level fast, she might lose it. She reached for his pants, but he grabbed her hand.

He bit her finger lightly, sending a jolt of desire through her. "I had no idea you were this impatient."

"We've waited for a while, don't you think?"

He sat up suddenly and flipped her onto her back. His leg settled between hers, effectively pinning her to the mattress. So much for her being in charge. Not that she minded. Seeing him in charge made her belly flip.

He kissed below her left ear. "Doesn't mean we should rush." He continued kissing her along the edge of her jaw while a hand lazily played with the strap of her bra.

Zelda arched up towards him and he grunted. She smiled. He wasn't as controlled as he was acting after all. She reached a hand around and laced her fingers through his hair. She gave a light tug and he kissed her mouth, understanding the silent command.

"I need you now," she said.

"Not yet."

"I'll kill you."

"No, you won't." He started moving south, and she knew he was right.

Zelda got lost in the sensation as Dylan undressed and explored her body. Soon, she saw stars behind her eyelids.

Dylan crawled back up and kissed her. "Better?"

"Much." She reached for his pants again. "But I want more."

He got up on his knees and gave her just that.

In what felt like both an eternity and a blink of an eye later, she lay on top of him in a tangle of sheets, their bodies pressed together.

She turned her head on his shoulder and kissed him again. "I love you."

"I think you're riding high on euphoria right now. How do I know it's not just gratitude?"

She lightly punched his side. "Shut up. You know it's not. And you're supposed to say it back."

He laughed. "But how will you know if *I'm* genuine?"

"Dylan."

"I'm kidding." He kissed her. "I love you, Zelda, and I always will."

She pulled him closer and knew that she was finally home where she belonged.

OTHER BOOKS

THE BELGRAVE LEGACY

SHORT STORY COLLECTION

UNMOORED

ACKNOWLEDGMENTS

I would like to first thank my friends, family, and readers for supporting my writing.

Special shout out to my magical cover artist: Jennifer Munswami (JM Rising Horse Creations).

Important note: authors live on reviews. And so, I ask you, my wonderful reader, to leave a review on your favorite retailer, and reccomend this book to your friends.

If you want to be kept in the loop about all my future publishing endeavors, subscribe now at zarahoffman.com/subscribe.

ABOUT THE AUTHOR

Zara Hoffman is a college student and has been writing since she was eight years old. She spends most of her time doing homework and writing new stories because if she didn't, her head would likely explode. Her books are for young adults and the young at heart. After all, growing up is overrated.

www.zarahoffman.com
zarahoffman@zarahoffman.com